Eating Jesus

Elaine Marney

Lipstick Publishing
www.lipstickpublishing.com

Lipstick Publishing,
118 Dewar Street,
Dunfermline, Fife.
Scotland KY12 8AA
www.lipstickpublishing.com
admin@lipstickpublishing.com

This paperback first edition 2006
First Published in Great Britain by
Lipstick Publishing December 2006

ISBN: 1-904762-33-6
ISBN: 9781904762331

A catalogue record for this book is available
from the British Library.

A man's dying is more the survivors' affair than his own.

Thomas Mann
'The Magic Mountain'

Dedication

To Charlotte and Jimmy for inspiration and ideas; to Chris, Catherine, Calum and Euan for love and support.

To all the good women of Brigton and the Gorbals, who are holding it all together; to any good men that are by their side.

Chapter One

"**W**ell, fuck you all then!"

He was standing in the doorway of the pub. He could see the Ulster flags hanging limp - the still air made it appear that, indeed, they had surrendered. Facing him were a sweating mass of Orangemen, collars loosened, ties stuffed in pockets. The younger ones had the Red Hand of Ulster flag draped over their shoulders like a cape, the corners tied under their chins. The women were still wearing their white hats with the Orange lily, despite the heat and humidity.

He felt his words create a creeping tension from the doorway, like an uneasy Mexican wave. Some of the men were staring at their hands, tables, anything other than him: they would tell the Polis they saw nothing of course. Others were being watched by their womenfolk – their faces said don't get involved; don't end up in jail, not tonight of all nights.

It was the Saturday before the Twelfth of July. Everyone in the pub – except him - had been in, or had followed, the Orange Walk that day. He could remember a time when the drum and flute had become one with his own throbbing pulse, his own heartbeat. When he was only five, he and his pals would play at apprentices and would take turns at dying to protect their families from the baddies, from the Papists. He too had wanted to guard old Derry's walls.

But love had changed him, had made him see that it was all a pile of macho, meaningless shite. Yet they still thought he was one of them. He took a deep breath and filled his lungs with the smoky air.

"And fuck King Billy as well, ya bunch of fuckin trogs!"

As he knew it had to, the pub shifted from a wary expectancy to choking fury, enraged at such heresy. In the eyes of his brothers and sisters he was now a treacherous renegade – beyond *The Pale*. Guts churning, he knew that the only way to avoid total destruction was for him to run for it, get back into the Gorbals. They wouldn't follow him there.

He took advantage of a moment's growling confusion in the pub, and backed out of the double doors like a gunslinger in reverse. Already running, he could hear the men as they piled into the street.

Orders were barked out: "Get doon Tullis Street! Cut the cunt aff at the Green!"

The Green? They thought he was headed for the city centre, not the Gorbals. He had a chance. He raced past the tenements of Mill Street, past his own *close* mouth in Greenhead Street, and vaulted the railings in a surge of adrenaline.

Within seconds he was safe on the King's Bridge, which separated Brigton from the Gorbals.

He leaned over, hands resting on knees, steadying his trembling legs and desperately pulling air back into his lungs. He retched violently, spilling puke onto his trainers. His muscles gave in to gravity and he collapsed onto all fours. He could hear thunder. Or was it the sound of his own rushing blood?

He heard again the roar of the thunder, and felt the cooling rain seep through his shirt. He'd escaped, and he could never return. He belonged to his lover now, forever.

For the short time left that he had to live, he wouldn't know why he suddenly raised his head, but when he did, a boot smashed into his face.

"Ya fuckin' traitor! Did you think you'd get away with it?"

He recognised the voice and laughed without joy, lips pulled back over teeth.

His attacker turned and ran back towards Brigton.

He tried to roll over, to get to his feet – but something had gone wrong, he couldn't move, he was sundered from his limbs. Blood was in his mouth and his throat, blocking his windpipe. As the rain came down in torrents it pounded his face and penetrated his nose and mouth. His body wanted to repel this vicious communion of blood and water: he gagged, and felt more puke rise. In desperation, he tried to suck in air, only to add vomit to the deadly, throttling, concoction.

As his young life choked out of him, his last thoughts were of the one he loved.

Chapter Two

"It was revealed today that the youth found dead on Saturday, the 8th of July on King's Bridge, near Glasgow Green, was within yards of his family home in Bridgeton. Police believe that twenty-two year old university student Robert Lawrence, died as a result of a single blow from an attacker, as yet unidentified. Robert is believed to have spent some time in the Gorbals area in the weeks leading up to his death.

Police are appealing for witnesses. Anyone who saw this incident, or has any other information about this crime, should contact London Road Police Station on 0141 555 5555."

* * *

Carol Reid stiffened when she heard the news item on the car radio. So that was it. Private tragedy: public knowledge.

Robert. Her wee cousin. Auntie Sarah's boy. She'd only seen him half a dozen times in the last few years. He'd been living it up as a student and she'd been too busy being a solicitor. She'd never see him again.

Carol pulled in off the High Street and tried to find a parking space in the old buildings of Glasgow Royal Infirmary. There were no spaces, so she had to park at the modern building, only then to find that the ward she was heading for was at the other end of about eighty-six miles of gloomy corridors.

Years ago, when she had first gone to Glasgow University, the self confidence of her fellow students had for a while completely undermined her own. They were from well-off families, from affluent suburbs like Bearsden or wealthy city areas like Pollokshields. For the first few weeks it was all she could do not to curtsey to them. Then she gradually relaxed and started seeing them as individuals, some a good laugh, some a pain in the arse. Even if they did all have shiny skin and robust frames, with the open smiles of those with unshakeable self-esteem, the Officer Class.

But the people passing her now in the hospital corridors, East Enders like herself, were the cannon fodder. The women had skinny pinched faces, or red bloated ones. There were a few who, she could tell, would have been good looking in their day. But that day had been a short one. If they'd been born into the middle classes they would have become handsome in their later years. For these women, however, years of poverty and deprivation had hardened their jaw line into defiant rigidity. When Carol looked in their eyes she saw no expression at all, not because the women had no feelings, but that life had taught them it was better to conceal them from the world.

The men were the same, walking alongside their womenfolk, but at least a foot away, with no parts of their bodies coming into contact. Where

Carol grew up, if a man showed too much affection he was regarded as weak, daft, a bit of a 'jessie', even if the object of his fondness was his wife, his girlfriend or even his children.

All this thinking had made her forget the ward number. Was it eighteen or eight? As eight was nearer she decided to try that first. As soon as she walked in, she knew she was in the right place. Ward eight was full of young men, the oldest ones being in their early twenties. They were all in various states of undress, some wearing shorts with no tops, others in trackie bottoms, not many in pyjamas. They looked like they had just been in one big communal rammy. Nearly every boy had black eyes and swollen lips and most had their wrists in plaster. Some were on a drip, or had other tubes coming from their body and into machines or bags of fluid. One sleeping boy had both legs in traction, although he was otherwise unmarked.

As she looked around, she heard the familiar voice.

"Miss Reid! Miss Reid! Whit you doin' here?"

It was coming from a bed near the window.

"John! It's you I've come to see. What happened to you?"

She went over to his bed, sat in the chair beside him. He had no other visitors.

"Got chased out the dancin' by two guys wi' swords."

John was in a right mess. He had lint pads

7

down one side of his face and his right arm was in a stookie, from his knuckles to his shoulder. He was topless and his body was covered in bruises and scratches.

John McFarlane, like Carol, was from Brigton. In fact his family had lived in the next street to hers. She could remember him as a wee baby in a tatty pushchair, getting hurled up the street by one of his many white-haired sisters, who looked no older than Carol, and she was only seven. With his pale blonde hair and big blue eyes he'd looked like an angel, or one of the paper water babies that she kept in a book of scraps. Now he was a sometimes client of Carol's, although nothing worse than breach of the peace and shoplifting. She hoped he wasn't moving up a league. He was only twenty.

"What were you getting chased for?"

"Shagged one of their birds. She fancied me. Couldnae let her down."

She studied the generous lover in front of her. He was about five feet five, a skinny wee runt. He still had pure blonde hair, but it was badly needing a scrub: his once spun-gold locks were plastered to his head on one side and on the other side stuck straight up, he looked like one half of a demented and tormented evil genius. He'd also lost one of his front teeth at some point.

"That was very gallant of you, John."

"That's just me but, intit? Her boyfriend's an ugly bastard anyway."

She laughed despite herself.

"Don't worry. It's sorted. Me an' ma cousin are gonnae get him when I get oot."

"Don't do that! Trust me, I'm a lawyer - you'll end up in the jail. "

"It's no' like I'm gonnae kill him or anythin'. My cousin might, but. He's mental. Anyway, if I don't get him back my cousin said he'd batter me … for being a prick and a shitebag."

She decided to change the subject.

"John, I've got a few things here."

She emptied a carrier bag onto his bed: a couple of crossword puzzle books, some chocolate and a few cans of coke.

"Aw Miss Reid, that's fuckin' brilliant of you, so it is. Naebody else has been up to see me, never mind brought me stuff."

Carol felt uneasy. She was no Florence Nightingale. She had been looking for him anyway, and had tracked him down to the hospital. Better to put him straight.

"John, your Probation Officer told me where to find you. I wanted to speak to you about something else … on a personal matter."

John sat up in bed, as much as he could with all his injuries. He looked very serious. Carol knew she shouldn't be doing this. She was also very much aware, that she was going beyond the bounds of acceptable client/solicitor relations.

But her mammy had sent her. And she feared Irascible Annie's wrath if she came back without the required information.

"It's about my cousin Robert …"

"Oh, aye, I was sorry to hear aboot Rab, Miss Reid, but I didnae really have anythin' to do with him …"

"It's OK John, I know you weren't pals or anything, and I'm not asking you to get involved in the murder enquiry."

John looked relieved at this. The Polis made him nervous.

"It's just that you've got such a big family, one of them must have been at school with him."

"Aye, my big sister Lizzie was in his class at school. She used to pure fancy him but then she clocked onto the fact that he was a … em … snob. Sorry Miss Reid, no offence like."

"It's OK John. But did any of your big sisters keep in touch with him in any way?"

John had been taking a swig out of one of the cans. The last question seemed to take him by surprise, or maybe he just swallowed the wrong way. At any rate, he coughed and spluttered, and Carol reached in her pocket for a hankie to help him wipe away the fizzy brown fluid that was coming out of his nose.

"Naw. They didnae mix in the same social circles, so to speak."

"Right, OK then. I'll tell you the reason I'm asking. We know that Robert had a girlfriend, and that he was going to see her in the Gorbals when he was attacked. The Polis let it slip but they won't give us any details. We just want to talk to her, that's all. I thought you might know something about it."

"A girlfriend … Rab Lawrence?"

"I know he was quiet, but even quiet ones get girlfriends John. His ma thinks maybe she was a Catholic and that's why he was hiding her away."

John was looking shady.

"I don't want involved Miss Reid. The Polis an' all that – nightmare. An' I don't know anythin' about a girlfriend, I swear to God I don't. Anyway, the Gorbals is outside my territory, how'd I know what goes on there?"

Carol knew she was getting nowhere. Except maybe struck off.

"Never mind John, I'm sorry to bother you when you're not well. I better get back down the road. Try to stay out of trouble, right?"

"Couldnae promise that. But you could do me a favour?"

"What is it?"

"All my clothes are covered in blood, an' ma maw will no' come up with clean ones."

"Has the hospital not phoned her to come and collect you?"

"We huvnae got a phone. Anyway, my cousin told me she told him to tell me to get to fuck."

"Oh, right. So, what's the favour John?"

"Could I get a wee sub on ma Legal Aid? I need to get a taxi home. I'm no walkin' the streets in these clothes. Everybody'll know I got a doin'. I'll look like a right tit."

Carol went into her bag and gave him a tenner.

"Here, John. But don't mention it round the office, OK?"

"No bother, Miss Reid. Cheerio."

As she was putting her purse away she caught sight again of the sleeping boy.

"John, what happened to him over there? The red headed one with both his legs in a stookie?

"Aw, him? That diddy? The paper boy? He skited on shite. Never saw it for the bundle he was carryin'. He fell under his da's delivery van. Broke both his legs."

"What a shame for him."

"No way! We were in the same ambulance. He gret like fuck and stank the place oot. As if I didnae have enough to worry aboot! I had to get a Tetanus jag 'cos of that dobber."

She said her goodbyes again and was halfway up the ward when he called her back.

"Honest to God, Miss Reid. I don't know anythin' about any girlfriends. But I heard there's a Paki shop near you where you can get all sorts of information. You should ask in there, aye. I cannae mind the Paki wumman's name, but it sounds like a white name."

"Sue?"

"That's it, aye"

"She's not a Pakistani, she's an Indian."

John looked baffled by the distinction.

"Thanks anyway John. I'll give it a try."

As she walked back through the tunnels leading to the car park, her mind was full of all those young men in that ward; every one of them, even the paper boy, the victim of stupidity of some sort. As a lawyer, Carol had represented countless young males who had gone out of a weekend, not expecting trouble, but certainly embracing it when it came along. Those that survived eventually settled down when they got a bit older. Some, like Robert, didn't survive those dangerous years. John might make it. If he could survive his family.

She was just about to start the engine when her mobile phone rang. It was her mother.

"Carol, I've just been to see your daddy – he's in a terrible state!"

"What were you doing in Brigton?"

Annie now lived in Rutherglen, a few miles away from both Brigton and the Gorbals.

"I went to see Sarah and Dan. After I left their house – they're still shattered by the way – I thought I'd call in and see your dad."

"Mum! I thought we were having nothing more to do with him after the last time! D'you not remember what you said …"

"Aye, I remember fine – name a' heavens Carol, you can be right hard when you feel like it! I only wanted to check up on him – Mrs Quinn tellt me he'd gone downhill, but I wisnae expecting him to be as far gone as he is."

"What exactly is wrong with him?"

"He's away with it! The drink's finally puggled his brain."

"Huh! That was only to be expected."

"Carol hen, if you seen him, you wouldnae talk like this. He's filthy, his house is filthy – there was even a strange dog in it! I don't know who it belonged to."

An hour later, Carol and her mother were standing in her father's living room. The whole house reeked of stale drink, piss and fags. In the corner of the room was a bucket. In it floated crushed cigarette packets and lumps of green phlegm: Carol tried not to think about what they were floating in. She was struggling not to gag. When she and Annie moved about the room, the carpet made sooking noises against the soles of their shoes.

There was no food in the kitchen but the bin was overflowing with bottles and cans. In the sink were dishes which had not been washed for days, perhaps weeks, they were covered in dried vomit, as if some one had puked all over them as they lay there.

She barely recognised her father. The last time she saw him, he of course was drunk, but this time it wasn't alcohol that was affecting him. As her mother had warned her, he was filthy. Normally clean shaven, his face was somewhere under a greasy stubble. His gold rimmed glasses were missing, replaced by ones which had the legs held on by sellotape. He stank. His hair had been allowed to grow down to his shoulders in wispy strands. His trousers were a patchwork of stains.

He had broken his arm at some point. The plaster was dirty and grey: its bulk was the only way to distinguish it from his skin as his hands were the same colour. His fingernails were ragged, yellow with nicotine. He was wearing only one slipper. No socks.

Archie was sitting in his chair, staring straight ahead: he seemed to barely notice that he had any visitors, let alone his wife and daughter. The sound on his television was up full, but the noise didn't seem to disturb him. Annie switched it off.

"Archie, Archie, it's me, it's Annie – d'you no' know me? I was here to see you earlier. I brought Carol back with me!"

Annie spoke to her ex-husband in a loud voice, as if she was talking to someone on a bad phone line.

"Oh, hello hen. Could you put ma tea on - I'm starvin'. I don't know where my wife's away to."

"Oh my God!" Annie had tears in her eyes. "I should never have left him – I'm to blame for this!"

Carol felt the old frustrations welling up.

"Look, mum, this isn't your fault. He's gone senile – that's what's up with him. You said it yourself on the 'phone – it's the drink."

Even as she said this, she knew that her father was not drunk: he didn't look strong enough to drink. This being so, why all the cans and bottles? The fag packets in the bins were several different brands. She also wondered how he could have lost so much weight: his clothes were hanging off him.

"But look at this house! And where's all the ornaments I left him? The place is stripped bare! This wouldnae have happened if I'd been here!"

"Mum, I'm telling you - whatever happened here, you didn't do it."

The front door was pushed open, banging off the wall of the lobby. A man's voice was heard:

"Right then you auld cunt! Got a poke a' chips for you. Mind, you're only getting it if you've signed those books!"

The man nearly died when he burst into the living room and saw the two women; although it didn't take him long to get it together.

"So you're back then."

He was probably about forty, but could have been younger. Tall and skinny, he smelled of stale drink and unwashed clothes. Carol could tell by his bloated and purple face that he drank the cheap wine. His sunken eyes and flat nose looked like those of a boxer's who'd never won a fight. He'd a leather jacket on, scuffed at the collar and elbows, burst zip. It was of no particular colour, much like the wee dog that was with him.

'So you're back then' - what did he mean?

"Who are you?"

"I'm Tam. I look after your da."

With these words she recognised him. He wasn't wearing well.

"Look after him!"

Annie's guilt was now converted to rage and vented his way.

16

"Sponge off him more like – swine!"

"Mum, leave it!"

Carol nearly told her mother to sit down, but the chairs looked dodgier than the carpet.

"No, I'll no' leave it!"

Annie walked right up to Tam, her face less than an inch from his.

"You've been using this place as a shebeen! Taking advantage of a senile old man. I'm getting the Polis in!"

"Whit are you gonnae tell the Polis, darlin'? I collect his money for him an' get his messages. I don't know whit he does after that."

"Messages? There's no food in the cupboards."

"Maybe he's et them all."

"Don't come it with me – there's not a pick on him!"

Tam shrugged his shoulders, while shiftily looking round the room. Carol knew he was looking for her father's pension books: he wanted the week's money signed over to him for the price of a bag of chips.

"No' my fault"

Carol also knew that she would have a job getting him prosecuted for anything. Right then she would have killed him if she could have got away with it.

"Well, I'll tell you one thing, you jaikey scumbag: your party days here are over. We're taking his books and we're looking after him now. So you can fuck off back under your rock."

She was surprising herself. You could take the girl out of Brigton but not Brigton out of the girl.

"And pass the word on to your wee pals – you're all barred!"

"Terrible mooth on you for a lawyer, huv you no'? Onyway, it's no your hoose. Archie – tell her to shove it!"

Carol's father seemed confused by all the arguing. When he looked at Tam it was as if he had met him years before, but the meeting had been a painful one.

"It's no' your hoose hen."

"Hear that – he doesnae want you interferin'."

The remark about being a lawyer shook Carol. She hated to think this creep knew anything about her. Then she noticed her father's walking stick. It had a brass head: she wondered why it had not gone the way of the other saleable items in the house. She strode across the room and picked it up.

"Aye, I hear that. And do you see this!" She brandished the stick. "If you don't get out, the last thing you'll ever see is your brains on the carpet!"

Tam backed out of the room, his eyes tightening to nothing.

"I'm goin'! It's you that should be gettin' lifted by the Polis, you mad bitch."

He headed for the front door of the house. The dog, being a creature of instinct, was long gone. Before finally leaving, Tam called out:

"By the way, I take it you're no plannin' to

move in. Are you gonnae be guardin' him night and day?"

Carol ran down the lobby corridor and hurled the stick through the front door. He was gone.

* * *

"Well, I just don't see how you can be that concerned with muggers and rapists and cannae go and visit your own father."

Carol's heart sank – her mother had been visiting him again. She had been legally separated from him for a whole year and she was still susceptible to the patter. Carol, still a trainee solicitor, tossed her pile of witness statements onto her mother's settee and plumped down beside them. She had hardly been five minutes in the door.

"All virtue lies in detachment, mother."

"Don't get smart lady. It's your mammy you're talking to here."

"Well, mammy, I'm not interested in goin' to see daddy!" She softened her tone. "Anyway, he's one of these men that doesn't need a family. He's self contained – he's happy!"

"How do you know whether or no' he's happy!" Annie shifted the files onto the sideboard, whilst having a quick look to see if she recognised the names on the spines. "You've no' seen him since your graduation."

"Exactly – two years ago. If he wanted to see the pair of us, he'd have sent word long since!"

Carol reached for the remote control. It had been a long day and all she wanted now was to relax and watch a soap opera. Not to be in one.

Annie stood in front of the television. "He didnae send for us. I ran into him in the Main Street."

She decided not to give her opinion of her mother's fib, not to get embroiled in an argument.

"I'm absolutely positively under no circumstances goin' down to Brigton."

The next day, Saturday, she and her mother were sitting side by side on her father's settee. If he had been expecting them he had a funny way of showing it.

They hadn't been listening for noises when they had knocked at the door, but as they stood waiting they grew aware that it had somehow got quieter: there was a sort of surprised silence in the air. Then they heard footsteps in the lobby, but no one answered the door. Carol guessed that they were being viewed through the spy hole.

The footsteps scuttled away: they heard panicked voices and the sounds of beer cans and bottles clunking off each other. A quick clearing up was obviously in progress. After another knock, her father answered the door; the noises were still to be heard.

She was struck by how untidy he looked. When she was younger she remembered her dad had been very fussy about his appearance: she and Annie still joked about how he would always put on his safari suit when they went on holiday. He wasn't exactly dirty, but he had the crumpled appearance of some one who hadn't been to bed for a few days.

"Annie, pet. And Carol too! Come on in – are you stayin' long?"

"Good to see you father" she said as she marched past him towards the living room.

She knew it! He wasn't bothering his arse whether he saw them or not. When was her mother going to get out of cloud cuckoo land?

Two guys were in the living room, one of them putting the debris into carrier bags, the other staring out the window.

"This is ma wife and ma lassie. She's a lawyer, you know."

"P-p-p-p-pleased to meet you hen – S-s-s-s-sorry aboot the mess - cl ... c ... cl ... clearin' it up for youse."

This was said, eventually, by the short one. Although it was a warm day, he had zipped his green parka anorak up to his chin. Maybe it was to catch the drips, as the front of it was covered in cheap wine stains, with a few greasy ones throw in. He looked about fifty, but it was hard to tell. His way of talking, his nervousness, his bad squint, which his black NHS specs hadn't corrected, gave him the look of someone who had spent years in an institution of some sort. Carol felt sorry for him. She now and again came across his type, arrested for minor offences, harassed and harried from cradle to grave. But the taller one was trouble. He had a leather jacket on: it was perhaps brown in its day. It – or him – smelled of a wet dog. From the back, he looked younger than the other one. While his pal was apologising, almost it seemed for his very existence, he still kept looking out the window.

"Tam, ya ignoramus!" this was her father.

Tam turned round. He stared wordlessly at her,

with the type of cold, assessing look which she wished was an arrestable offence. She hoped her face was expressionless as she met his eyes.

"Tam disnae talk much. He's illiterate. A pape."

Tam shot such a look of distilled hatred at Archie that Carol couldn't help taking a step back. From where she was standing, she knew that neither her mother nor father could see his expression. She turned away from him and sat beside her mother, who was already on the settee. She wondered what his game was.

He spoke for the first time. "I'm gonnae take ma jacket off, Archie. I'm sweatin' like a whore here."

He was wearing a ripped, armless tee shirt; although he was skinny, the muscles on his arms were sinewy and tough-looking. He sat beside her, his right thigh tight against her left.

Shit, shit, shit! What were they doing here? She glanced sideways at her mother who was playing with her locket, a sure sign that she was nervous.

Her mother was trying to make some kind of small talk. Carol wasn't really listening, but Annie seemed to have found out that the short one was called Malky.

"Aye, missus, when I was put oot the hospital I was skipperin' roon Glasgow Cross for two years."

"Skipperin', Malky, what's that?"

Annie's tone was that of someone asking the Minister if he was in good health. Carol loved her for being nice to this wee man.

"Ma wife's never heard that expression Malky. She's had a sheltered life."

'Not when she was living with you, you clown,'

22

Carol thought.

"Skippering means living rough mum."

She felt, rather than heard, Tam's derisory snort.

As Malky and her parents kept up some sort of conversation, she looked round the room. Since her mother had left him, her father had definitely pared his life down to the bare essentials. Apart from one or two ornaments – gold cupped hands, and a glass fish with a gaping mouth, both throwbacks to the seventies – there was no fine detail to the room. She saw that the hands and the fish had only survived because they were being used as ashtrays. There was a layer of dust everywhere and the air was stale.

Tam finally spoke to her in a loud voice, whilst glancing over at Archie, to include him in what he was saying.

"Don't talk much, do you?"

"No, but …"

"Got to watch cunts like you."

She didn't answer him, but looked at her father, who looked away. She knew he'd heard Tam, and that he was ignoring her. So that's how it was these days. He'd become king of the heap, and couldn't afford to argue with his subjects over a daughter he never saw. Fair enough.

"C'mon mum." Carol kept her voice even, bantering almost. "We're going up the town, remember? We better get a move on, before the shops get mobbed."

Her mother stood up. They both still had their jackets on.

"I'll see youse to the door." Her father led them

23

along the lobby. There were a few bright patches where pictures had been.

"See youse later then," he said as her mother went ahead of her.

"No, you won't daddy," she replied.

Chapter Three

Sarah listened as the Minister praised her dead son.

"Hard working student ... gifted at maths ... former officer in the Boy's Brigade ..."

She couldnae fault the man: her son had been all these things, but these werenae important to her. They'd made her proud at the time, but she'd have loved him anyway, even if he'd been a dunce or a rogue.

Robbie, her wean, was murdered. Someone local, the Police said. How could that be? Who could do this to her? Brigton was a wee place, she thought she knew everybody. She thought she did.

The last time Sarah had been in the Linn Crematorium had been her own mother's funeral. Grannie Jean had aye said to her daughter to speak well of folk, be kind, if they were bad to you, and mind that you'll see your ain of them, in the end. She meant that bad folk aye died alone and unhappy. So that's what she'd done: she'd been kind, a good neighbour, and brought her boy up to be the same for bye. And where had it got her? Her son was murdered.

Mrs Quinn, a wee Irish buddy she knew, had told her that she was praying to Our Lady for the soul of Robbie. Sarah had been fair affronted, for she knew that nobody in this world could interfere with God's will. Judgement had been passed on her son. For all eternity. But then the old wife had meant well, so she'd thanked her all the same.

She felt her man move in the seat beside her – they were back where they started twenty two years ago – childless. When they died, they'd be forgotten. Her mother believed you would be minded by folk for being a good person, but nobody cared about that these days. These days they killed your wean one day and forgot it the next.

She'd been forty when she'd finally fallen pregnant, and been married for fifteen years. They'd rarely spoken about the fact they'd no weans. Dan wasn't one for talking about those kind of things - 'women's troubles'. He never cast it up to her, but then he never comforted her either. When Robbie finally arrived though, even he, Dan Lawrence, went soft: he took one look at the baby and burst into tears. She could remember the midwife staring at the two of them, both a bit past it, a pair of bubbly-jocks.

Robbie. 'Sweet Robin' she called him when she put him in his crib in the hospital: she remembered the name frae when she learnt about Robert Burns at the school. Her man asked her what kind of bloody name was that, and did she know many other Robins in Brigton? He was right of course so they christened him Robert, but when his father was out she called him Robbie.

When Robbie was born you were considered queer if you breast-fed your wean, but hers wasn't getting fed that powder stuff. When he was newborn she didn't sleep for eight nights and when she went home frae the maternity hospital she was stuck in the house for days – she couldn't feed him outside. She'd have got lifted by the Polis. Dan had the cheek to look embarrassed, and would have started, but she wasn't having that. She just tellt him, she wasn't going to start hiding ben the room from her own man, so if he didn't like to see her breasts as nature intended, then she'd make sure he never saw them again. She never got a cheep out of him after that.

Robbie. Her bonnie wee bairn. He'd stuck in at the school and didnae hang around corners, getting mixed up with hooligans. He was quiet, deep. She never knew the half of what was going on in his mind, but she trusted him. He was the only boy in his class to go to the University; he was coming out to be a Mechanical Engineer. He had one more year to go.

Robbie. She'd never see him again in this life. Her son was dead and she wished she was away to join him. Her whole existence was split into two lives: the one before, and the one after, Robbie died. Before, she had an ordinary life, a wee part-time job, a decent man, a clever son, a hope of grandweans in the future. Now she realised what a paradise she'd been living in.

After Robbie died, there was only pain. In her dreams, she'd wake up to see his good-looking, sombre face leaning over her, telling his mammy no' to greet, it was a mistake; it was some other guy that was murdered. Or she'd dream that he was a wee boy again: he'd dreepied the dykes and skint his elbows, and was licking the blood off his arms and showing her his scab. She'd reach out to cuddle him, and then she'd wake up again, for real this time. Was this what hell was like? Not fire and brimstone - just suffering and pain?

The coffin was disappearing behind the curtain. They were to stand to sing a hymn – the Twenty-third Psalm. Why was Dan still sitting there? For the first time in days, she looked straight at him, and felt ashamed. His head was down, he was shaking: his grief was inside him, torturing him in his silence. She should have known by now that the more he suffered the more he became like stone to the outside world, and even to his wife. How could he change now at his age? She felt so sorry for him. She looked away as he struggled to his feet.

The service was over. They had to line up in the doorway to speak to the folk who'd came. She had hoped to stand beside her man in this way at her boy's wedding. What had happened to the girl-friend? Robbie thought he was keeping her a secret, so Sarah had guessed the lassie was a Catholic. She'd have preferred the lassie to be a Protestant, for the sake of the weans, but she knew how headstrong Robbie was: if she'd made him choose she'd have maybe lost him. The Police would tell her nothing – the lassie 'whilst not a suspect was part of the ongoing investigation' – what did that mean? She was shaking hands now with the mourners. She couldn't speak, she could only think. For the first time ever, Dan was doing all the talking. Robbie's University pals were the last in the line up: some young fellas she only just recognised, and his pal Michael. Robbie had once accused his dad of being a bigot, but how could that be when he'd welcomed Michael into his home?

Michael had brought his sweetheart. Sarah could tell he loved her by the way he looked at her, and the way he was holding her hand. They looked well suited to each other, they had a future together.

"Mrs Lawrence, this is Josie, she's my ..."

The sight of them was too much for Sarah and she turned her face and closed her eyes. Could the young man no' see that if she tried to say even one word, her heart would burst and she'd greet so hard, they'd have to take her away?

When she felt more in control she opened her eyes. There was nobody there. She went out of the hall, along the corridor and into the open air. The coach was there, waiting to take the mourners to the purvey at the Orange Halls. Her sister, Annie, and her niece, Carol, were helping Archie up the steps. Poor old soul. Still, he'd been well warned

29

about the drink. And he'd had his life, not like Robbie.

The coach was packed, but most of the folk were of ages with her and her man. She saw the young couple hurrying down the hill, away from the funeral party. Surely they understood?

If they ever outlived their weans, they'd understand.

Chapter Four

When Carol heard she had been accepted for the Faculty of Law at Glasgow University her first thoughts were that she had an excuse to move out of the family home. After all, that's what students did. But she found the West End of Glasgow a bit scary: in the pubs the toilet walls were full of graffiti about anarchy and lesbian sex. Not that she was against lesbian sex or anarchy and she'd never tried either, but it was an awesome world for an eighteen year old from Brigton to suddenly find herself immersed in.

Instead she moved into a multi-storey flat in the Gorbals, set aside especially for university students. The main attraction of the Gorbals was that she knew her father would not go there, although he could have walked the distance from his home to hers in twenty minutes. Being Brigton born and bred, he disapproved of the Gorbals - too many Catholics.

Having been brought up in a noisy tenement, she loved her little flat on the eighteenth floor. She had always found the romantic notions associated with the tenements wearisome in the extreme. What tenement life in an old community like Brigton meant to her was a total lack of privacy; overwhelming pressure for men to conform to the hard drinking, hard-man image; women robbed of their full potential, subservient to their husbands and their homes.

She could not remember seeing any eccentric people around her where she grew up. Nobody was allowed to be.

She had privacy in the Gorbals. She liked the fact that she rarely talked to her neighbours: she knew they knew where she lived because when she got into the lift on the ground, someone always pressed her floor number without asking her. This silent acknowledgement was enough for her. Just like Brigton, there was crime, drugs, wife beating, but up on the eighteenth floor, with the view of the city and the Cathkin Braes, it all seemed to be somewhere else, not in the world she had created, in her two rooms with separate kitchen and bath-room.

As a trainee solicitor, she was paid little more than a teenager on a government scheme but when she finally started earning she felt ridiculously pretentious living in a council flat. For the first time in her life, she was burdened with prosperity. She didn't want to leave the Gorbals but she couldn't stay where she was. Then one day, as she was walking along to the subway on the way to work, she noticed workmen clearing some waste ground. Enquiries were made: the council was subsidising the building of private flats in the Gorbals, with the intention of keeping those with spending power in the area, part of the 'regen-eration' process. Within a year she'd moved into a three-bed roomed flat and installed a lodger, Patsy, to help with the mortgage. Patsy was a legal secretary in the firm where Carol worked. She didn't have many faults, but one of them was never replacing the milk if she used the last.

Or at least that's the excuse Carol would use, if she was asked why she was in the local 'dairy' at half past eight on an August Saturday morning, trying to pluck up the courage to play super sleuth. She'd made the mistake of telling her mother about John's tip, and she'd been pestering her for weeks. What finally made Carol agree to approach Sue was the threat Annie made of going down there herself. God knows how that would have ended up.

Sue was at the till as usual. That wasn't her full name, but that's what she was known as by her customers. She had come from India as a young bride thirty years ago, unable to speak any English; she'd arrived in February and was chilled to the bone, her native clothing totally inappropriate for the Scottish weather. Even now, years later, she still wore the traditional dress of a Sikh woman – her only compromise was that over the colourful silks and spun-gold threads she wore a Fair Isle jumper.

The Sikh religion values fearless courage, as a bunch of young counter jumpers found out to their cost when, as they were loading their pockets with fags, Sue reached under her top layer of clothing and pulled out her kirpan, a traditional short

33

sword, worn by all Sikh women. There is a difference between traditional and ceremonial, the difference in this instance being half a foot of curved steel, sharpened and now unsheathed. Nobody ever jumped the counter again.

"Carol, hen, you're no' lookin' too good. Up the dancin' to all oors?" Sue had never learned proper English: she spoke Glaswegian.

Carol leaned on the counter, wondering what to say next.

"I was on a date."

Lies. Why did she say that?

"A date? Is that a new man in your life then?"

"Em, no. After five minutes, I realised I didn't really like him."

"Whit are you like Carol! How do you no' settle down with a nice man to look after you?

"I never meet any nice men – I only ever meet lawyers and clients. I don't know which is worse: middle class nitwits or petty criminals."

"Glasgow's a big city. There must be some suitable men."

"But all the interesting ones are spoken for. Anyway, I want to ask you something."

"Aye, whit is it?"

Carol's nerve was failing her. This was ridiculous. What was she going to say? 'I hear this shop is a hotbed of information, that you know everything about everybody, so where is my cousin's girlfriend?'

"Have you got any fresh orange juice?"

"It's in the fridge, near where you got the milk."

As she moved to the back of the shop, Carol heard someone else come in. She glanced round, to see a very pale young woman, about twenty, with long red hair. Carol sneaked another glance at the girl as she moved towards the fridge and lifted a carton of yoghurt: she was deathly white, clearly suffering from some kind of illness. The girl seemed to sense she was being observed: she turned to Carol, whose first response had been to smile sheepishly, embarrassed at being caught gawping, but when she met the girl's eyes the smile faded. They were pale green, only a little darker than her skin, which together gave her a luminous look, like a Pre-Raphaelite corpse.

Sue called out to her.

"How are you getting on, Josie?"

"Fine."

Sue served the girl in silence. When she left the shop, Sue spoke to Carol in a low voice.

"That poor lassie. Her man was killed a few weeks ago. She's no' been right since then."

"What happened to him?"

"He was attacked. They never caught anybody but they say the Orange people were after him."

"Orange people?"

"Yes. People who arenae Catholics. Whit are they called again?"

Sue had heard of the religious divide in her adopted city, but being a Sikh, found it hard to see a difference between the two. If she was pushed, she would have to admit that all Glaswegians looked the same to her: like the food, pale and bland. The girl who had left the shop was paler than most.

Carol, meanwhile, was trying to remember how to breathe. And to resist the urge to jump the counter and give Sue a big kiss. She'd heard about the sword incident.

"Sue, how do you get to know all of these things?"

"I get to hear all the gossip. People sometimes forget I can understand whit they're saying, so they chatter away right in front of me. That's one pound forty-five."

Carol nearly threw the money at her, in her rush to catch up with the girl, what had Sue called her – Josie? She started walking along the road, in the direction of the flats. On the way she almost tripped over someone. It was her, Josie. She was sitting on the ground against a wall.

She knelt down beside the girl, touched her gently on the shoulders.

"Josie."

The girl lifted her head. Again, those eyes, more red-rimmed this time.

"Do I know you?"

"No. Did you know Robert Lawrence?"

"Rob's dead."

So, here she was, the mystery woman, delivered up to her in Sue's shop. John would have been impressed. Yet as Carol looked at her, she knew she was familiar. The Gorbals was such a wee place really. Carol had passed this girl a few times in the street, and probably seen her in Sue's shop before. If only she'd been with Robert one of those times. Maybe if Carol and her had met properly, they could have been friends. Carol could even have worked on her family, starting with Annie, to make them accept this girlfriend, this love of Robert's.

But it was all summed up in those two words: Rob's dead. She should have taken more notice of him when he was alive, instead of wrapping herself up in her own not very special world. Wee Robert. The baby of the family. The Wean. She couldn't help him now. But she could help Josie.

"I know. My name's Carol Reid. I was - I am - his cousin. What about you? You're not looking well."

Josie struggled to her feet. "I was just a bit dizzy. OK now."

But she wasn't. Josie swayed and grabbed hold of the wall.

"It's the smell from the butcher's shop. It always gets to me."

"Look, I'll help you up to your house. Give me your bag. I'll carry it for you."

Carol took Josie's small bag of groceries and offered her arm. Josie slid hers into it.

"Thanks, I live up the flats."

As they passed the shop window, Carol didn't

notice one of the butchers stop what he was doing and peer through the glass at them.

Once out of the lift and in the landing at Josie's front door, Carol handed her bag back to her.

"I don't want to rummage about for your keys."

"Thanks. You've been a great help."

The girl seemed undecided about what to do next.

"So you're one of Rob's family then?"

"Yes, did he never mention his big cousin Carol?"

"No."

"Oh, right. Well, I'd hardly seen him over the last few years."

"I've got photos. Come in and I'll show you them."

Josie opened the front door and led Carol down the long hall into the living room. Carol, knowing this was a student's flat, had expected it to look like hers once did: protest posters on the wall, ancient furniture covered by ethnic print fabrics, and joss stick holders on the mantelpiece. Her flat had been typical of someone who had just left home and was experimenting with who they were and what they wanted.

This flat, or as much as she had seen of it, had a more permanent look to it. The living room was rust and cream coloured; the curtains matched the fitted carpet and the two settees blended in with the colour scheme; the occasional tables came from the same set, and the pictures on the wall had frames on them. The place looked grown-up.

"I'll look out those photos. Would you like a tea or coffee?"

"A coffee would be great. I take lots of milk. Here, take this pint I got at Sue's – I'll buy another one later. In fact, show me the kitchen and I'll put the kettle on. You should be resting."

The girl smiled at her.

"How did you know my name?"

"I heard Sue say it. Then she told me about your boyfriend, so I guessed who you were. I've been looking for you. I live in the Gorbals as well- in the new builds over at Cumberland Street."

"Well, neighbour from the posh flats, the kitchen's through there. I'll take a herbal tea."

In the kitchen, Carol made the herbal tea first, as it took a few minutes to infuse. She looked around the kitchen while she was waiting. Like the other room, this one had been planned. The storage jars, mugs, trays and even the kettle and the clock had the same trendy pattern on them. So far, everything she'd seen suggested to Carol that Josie had bought everything all at once, and not bit by bit as she could afford it.

What she did notice was that the glass storage jars were empty, and when she opened up the fridge to put the remains of her pint of milk in, it was bare.

"No wonder she collapsed", thought Carol "the daft waif's been starving herself."

Back through in the living room, Josie was sitting on the couch with a small pile of photographs on her knee. Carol's heart went out to the girl: in the middle of her lovely, well ordered home, there she sat, desperate to look through photographs of her dead boyfriend with a complete stranger, anything to keep him a little bit alive.

She placed the mugs on coasters on a lamp table and sat beside the girl. The first photograph she was handed was of a beach scene: she could tell it was Scotland, because although the sun was shining, the young man and women were wearing jackets. The photographer must have been lying on the ground as the shot was taken from below: the young woman, Josie, had jumped onto the back of Robert. Her eyes were screwed up and her mouth was open with laughter. Carol could almost hear the squeals of delight. Robert was more serious. He was caught off guard by the surprise attack of the girl: although he was smiling over his shoulder at her, observing her hilarity, he looked a little awkward.

"I was closest to Robert when he was a wee boy. I saw him nearly every day, back then. He'd grown into a good looking guy."

"Yes, although he never thought so. He was the least vain person I'd ever met."

"Now that you mention it, I can remember him coming out of the chemist's at Brigton Cross, oh, years ago. I think I was waiting for a bus. He had a carrier bag, and he had to pass these wee girls, who started giggling and trying to get his attention. It was dead obvious they fancied him. His face was beetroot red, but he never looked at them once, all the way up to his close. He was always a bit shy of girls."

"Maybe those self-same wee girls know the Brigton scumbag that murdered Rob."

"What makes you think it was a Brigton person?"

"He was chased out of a pub in Brigton. He was running back here when they caught him. They gave Rob a kicking and left him to choke on his own vomit. Then they scuttled back to Brigton."

Josie's face had been blank when she talked of the murder. Suddenly, she lost control, and she started to sob.

"He was coming back to me! They killed him! He was going with a Catholic and they couldn't handle it! Even at his funeral!"

Carol reached for the girl, but she jumped from the couch and ran into the adjoining kitchen, leaving her sitting there, awkward and embarrassed. Should she go after her? Much to her surprise, she'd achieved what she'd set out to do – to find Robert's girlfriend. All she had to do now was report in to her mother and let Annie and Sarah take over. Shouldn't she just go home?

The decision as to whether she should leave quietly was made for her. She heard the front door opening: it took a while to close, making her think that more than one person had walked through it. Sure enough, she heard footsteps in the hall, low voices and a jangling of small change: men. More trouble.

"Josie! It's only me and Mick! Where are you?"

This was delivered in a hearty roar, but as they came down the hall, the men spoke quietly to one another, in another tone entirely.

"You're pallier with her than me, for fuck's sake. Can you no' get through to her?"

This was from the one who had called out.

"She'll no' listen to me either! What about Uncle Peter? Should I try him?"

"That bastard! For fuck's sake Mick. He chucked her oot the hoose, called her a wee hoor in the middle of the street."

"I know, I know, OK. See but, I wish your ma was still alive, Jim. This is a woman's thing …"

The voice trailed off as they came into the living room and saw Carol. The one who had spoken last said:

"You the Polis? Has she no' answered enough?"

He was in his twenties, tall and broad. Big, like a navvy, big hands, big chest, big legs. The sort of big that you get, not from working out, but from just being born like that. He had a pale face, dark hair and dark eyebrows, with those green eyes, same as Josie.

"Hold on, Mick. Let the lassie alane. She's no' a cop."

This was the one who had called out. Jim, was it? He looked like a smaller version of the other, same features and colouring, but where the bigger guy looked awkward and clumsy; this one looked to Carol to be compact and relaxed in himself. Same pale green eyes. Maybe it was because they both looked like Josie, but she felt she knew him from somewhere.

"I saw you. That's how I'm here. I couldnae get away, or I'd have come out to talk to youse earlier on. I'm on my tea break. Josie's my wee sister."

That's where she knew him from. She didn't recognise him without his overalls. He was one of the butchers from the local shop.

"You're looking for Josie? She's in the kitchen. She's a bit upset. I don't think she's too well."

They both sat on the couch facing her.

"She's up the duff."

This was blurted out by Mick. As soon as he said it, his face flushed red as he glanced at Jim. Carol could have kicked herself. Of course she was! That explained the fainting fits and the pasty face.

"That's no' public knowledge yet, sweetheart," said Jim. "Keep it to yoursel' for now, please eh?"

"Sure. I met Josie in the dairy. When she took not well outside I thought I'd better help her home."

"That was good of you. Is your name Carol, by the way? Live in the yuppie flats?"

God! First Sue, now this guy. What was it with

those shops, were they a secret MI5 base? Did they have a file on everybody? The suggestion that she was a yuppie grated on her but she decided not to make a big thing of it.

"Yes, how did you know that?"

"You came into my work to get some wee busty blonde bit."

She looked at him blankly.

"I was boning out in the back shop and I seen you. Your pal was yatterin' away to the woman I work with and you came to look for her cos' she'd got your keys."

Realisation dawned. A few weeks ago, Patsy had been on a half day and had left her keys at home. She borrowed Carol's and had promised to go straight back home. When Carol arrived four hours later there was no one in. A neighbour mentioned she'd seen Patsy in the butchers twenty minutes ago, talking to the assistant. Carol went to investigate and she was still there.

"It was a Tuesday," added Jim.

Carol had started to feel flattered that she'd been remembered. This last remark set off warning bells.

"Don't worry, I'm no' a stalker."

No, just a mind reader.

"The reason I know it was a Tuesday because that's the gaffer's day off. Wee Mags isnae allowed to talk to customers, so when Frew's no' in she runs riot. Serves about one customer an hour, an' gives everybody her life history. Ahh, here she is!"

Josie had come out of the kitchen, smiling.

"Jim, why are you not at your work?"

"I'm on a break. I met Mick in the lift. He's up to see how you are, sweetheart."

Jim's voice, when he spoke to his sister, was gentle, concerned. The Mick one was quiet for now, watching Josie, waiting for a response. She, in turn, looked at Carol.

"I'm sorry for abandoning you there. I hope these two galloots have been nice to you."

Just for a moment, the mood of the room had looked like it was going to revert to tragedy, but this expression of Josie's lightened it. Mick smiled for the first time.

"And did you introduce yourselves to Carol properly, or have you just been chatting her up all this while?"

Josie was trying very hard to pull herself together.

"This is my brother Jim and my cousin Michael. They take turns to come up to dirty my nice cream carpet."

"Well, if you looked after yoursel', we would-nae need to annoy you every day. Anyway, Mick's a student. He's got nothin' else to do with his time."

"That's right." Mick smiled at Josie.

She moved over and kissed the top of his head.

"Michael's my best pal," she explained to Carol.

"What about me?" asked Jim.

"You cheeked me up too many times when I

45

was wee to be my best pal."

"Cheeked *you* up? The reverse is more like it!"

Carol waited to see if Josie would mention her being related to Robert. Instead, she went back through to the kitchen to make more coffee. Maybe Josie didn't trust her self-control to stay intact if she brought his name up again.

Jim glanced down at the photographs which were still lying on the couch.

"I see Josie was showing you her photos."

He looked straight at Carol.

"Yes, I'm Robert's cousin."

"Well, whit do you make of that! Mick here was at university with him."

"Were you?"

"Yup. Worked on the roads with Jim's da here for a few years. Too much like hard work so I went to Uni instead."

"Robert was an engineer, so you'd be as well?"

"Mechanical. Rab wanted to design aircraft. Me too, in fact. We were thinking of applying to Boeing when we graduated next year. Josie was gonnae come too. Don't think I'll bother now, but."

Josie came back through from the kitchen with two steaming mugs of coffee.

"I've got milk for a change. Carol brought some in with her."

"I'll just need to gulp this down, toots, and then get back to work," said Jim, "Frew's in a huff, so I better not cross him. Somebody lent him a season ticket for Ibrox today and he had to cancel 'cos

46

Wee Mags phoned in sick."

"He's a Rangers fan, then," Carol commented vaguely, as she stood up to leave.

"He'd paint his grass blue if he could. Won't let his weans watch 'The Sound of Music' in case the nuns corrupt them."

"Sounds like someone I know," said Carol, "thanks for the coffee, Josie. I better get down the road."

"I'll see you to the door," said Josie.

When Josie opened the door to let Carol out, she put her hand on her arm.

"What did you mean, you'd been looking for me. How did you know about me? The Police?"

"The Police wouldn't tell us anything about you. My Aunt Sarah had guessed that Robert had a girlfriend. Apparently he'd started looking after his appearance and getting secretive about his activities. Classic signs that he was going with someone. She wants to meet you, you know."

"I like you, Carol, and if we kept in touch that would be good. But only with you, not with the Lawrence clan."

"What do you mean?"

"What I mean, is that I don't want you to tell Rob's mother that you met me or know anything about me."

"But what about the baby? Don't you think she'd like to know she was going to be a granny?"

"How do you know about the baby?"

"Your cousin said."

Josie sighed in frustration.

"That galloot. Anyway, I still don't want anything to do with Rob's parents, so it would be a kindness not to tell them, don't you think?"

"You're talking about my aunt and uncle. They're good people."

"Look, Carol, I don't want to argue with you. But that's how it is. Will you respect my wishes?"

"I will. But here's my phone number, Josie. Give me a call and come up some evening for a coffee or tea or something."

What would she tell Annie?

Chapter Five

Patsy came up to Carol's desk with a cup of coffee and a fairy cake with a plastic skeleton embedded in the icing.

"Here, spoil yourself. Your eleven o'clock's making her way up from the lobby, so I thought you'd like a wee treat to give you strength. I put the file on your desk this morning: *Somner against Strathclyde Police*."

Carol looked at the cake. She was trying to cut down on sweets, to fit into a slinky number in time for Christmas, but the thought of the grief she was about to go through for this crappy case brought on a sugar craving.

The Somner case. Gavin had landed it on her yesterday, which made her automatically suspicious. She read the last letter to Mrs Somner, written the week before by that bloody ineffectual idiot.

Sometimes, in her darker moments, Carol felt surrounded by middle class twits, who lived up to every stereotype going. Gavin Ogilvie, the Junior Partner at Fraser, Templer and Quinn (or F.T.Q. as Patsy gleefully called it), was determined to keep the side up. He was a perfect example of the triumph of confidence over competence. She was going to go through to see him.

Carol and most of the other solicitors shared a

large open-plan office, but Gavin had his own room. To get to it, she had to go through Reception. Mrs Somner had arrived and was waiting expectantly. She'd been told to ask for Carol, and was looking out for her.

"Hello, pet. My day in court's come round at last, eh?"

"Yes, Mrs Somner, a big day for you tomorrow. Would you excuse me a second? I have to consult a colleague about your case."

"That'll be Mr Ogilvie? Don't worry pet, he's got it all under control. That was the very words he used."

Carol twitched almost imperceptibly. Out of the corner of her eye she saw Patsy move from behind the Reception Desk.

"Will I show Mrs Somner to the Boardroom, Miss Reid?"

"That would be great Patsy. I won't be long with Mr Ogilvie."

Carol covered the short corridor to his room in three paces. She knocked and entered right away – she didn't ask to come in because she wasn't going to give him the opportunity to say no.

Gavin's desk was facing the door, so that he had his back to the window. The window started at the ceiling and went practically all the way down to the floor, giving him a great view when he swivelled round on his sumptuous leather chair with adjustable everythings. The chair on the other side of the desk was comfortable enough, but half the size of Gavin's. When you sat on it on bright sunny days you could only see Gavin in silhouette, although he could see you perfectly well. Carol knew what he was up to and wondered just how tiny this guy's dick could be.

As she stood inside the door she heard the plink-plonk of Gavin logging on to the Internet. He was looking up the 'improve your golf swing' web sites again. He did this every day: with one other exception, it was the only thing he used the computer for, as he got Patsy to do all his typing and he didn't know how to access the accounts. He wasn't very computer literate at all, and in fact had never realised that the Internet search engine contained a three week history of all the sites he'd ever visited. Whenever he was out the office Patsy checked it, to see what he'd been up to. Golf in the mornings, the more explicit searches *after* office hours. Even Gavin had some level of discretion.

It took him a few seconds to notice Carol and when he did, he moved the mouse across his desk.

"Aha Carol, just looking up the Law Reports."

Carol walked over to his desk, peered round the monitor into the screen. It was blank.

"Anything exciting, Gavin?"

Gavin reached down and pressed the power button on the computer.

"Oh, pretty boring really, same old thing. Better switch off and get down to making money."

"You look a bit flushed Gavin, feeling the heat?"

"At this time of year?"

"Another thing Gavin, did you press 'Shut Down' before you switched the power off?"

"Shut Down? I turn the computer off the same way every evening. Surely that's the purpose of the 'off' button?"

"Gavin," Carol purred, "You silly man, you'll corrupt your files. When you turn the computer back on, it'll go automatically to the last site you visited. Here, let me show you, I wanted to look at last week's judgements anyway."

"No, really!" This was practically a squeak. "I'll see to it later. Must get on. Why did you come in, anyway?"

Torturing him had calmed her. Slightly.

"I've got Mrs Somner in the boardroom, working out how to spend her three grand damages."

"Now, give me some background, Mrs Somner?"

"The Mrs Somner whose Road Traffic proof is on tomorrow?"

His face was still a blank.

"The Mrs Somner who is suing Strathclyde Police for damages? Despite the fact that Police Officers are generally regarded as having protection of suit when doing their duty, and in this case probably quite rightly so? The Mrs Somner who went into the back of the car in front, the driver of the said front car braking sharply because he heard sirens, but, as I note from a precognition, now cannot remember if it was a Police car or an

Ambulance that crossed his path? The Mrs Somner who expects to get three grand damages, notwithstanding the fact she was three steps away from the primary cause, had no injuries and suffered no loss of earnings?"

"And your point, Carol?"

"The Mrs Somner, Gavin, to whom you sent a letter last week, containing the words, and here I quote, *'bound to win'*?"

"Ahh well, there we have it. Positive mental attitude."

He held up his hands in front of his face, his fingers the shape of a square, with his fingertips touching, as if he was looking through some kind of viewfinder.

"*See* yourself winning the proof, Carol, *see* the Sheriff finding for our client. Positive Visualisation, that's what you've failed to nurture, Carol."

This guy definitely was beset with delusions of adequacy.

"Seeing as she's in now, and she believes that you've got it 'all under control', another quote, verbatim this time, perhaps you would like to speak to her?"

"Any other time, I'd have a quiet word, settle the nerves all round, but I'm rather busy. You could surely handle this one on your own, without me this time Carol?"

Was he smarter than she'd given him credit for? Deliberately provoking her, or just a genuinely arrogant fool?

"I thought you might be the best one to explain that the firm will most likely not be seeking any payment from her."

"What?"

At least it sounded like 'What?' He was making the same gurgling noises as the guy in 'Midnight Express' when he got his tongue bitten off.

"You see, Gavin, this is the same Mrs Somner who does not qualify for Legal Aid and whose case you took on, on a speculative basis, who should really be paying in the region of £2,000 for the amount of work carried out on her behalf but who we can't charge, because (a) we'll probably lose, and (b) even if she wins, could you imagine what the Law Society would say if we took most of her compensation in fees?"

"Why bring the Law Society into everything Carol?"

"Because, Gavin, they *will insist* that solicitors maintain a certain level of professional competence and integrity. I can predict potential Law Society complainants, and this client bears the hallmark of one, especially if she starts waving your letter about."

Money was one of the few things that moved Gavin. Another was the idea of the Law Society investigating his practices. Carol studied him. He had, as her mother would say, 'a face like a flittin'.

"Anyway Gavin, I can see you're busy, must get on. Ciao"

She managed to suppress her giggles until she got to reception, and then made a noise like a balloon being let down.

Patsy came up to her.

"I've given her another cup of tea and a bourbon cream – no point in wasting the good biccies on clients. Hey, you've been tormenting Gavin again. That's the only time you smile in the office. What did you do to him?"

"God bless him. I don't really take pleasure in baiting him, but then again it does get me through the day."

"Oh, I know. What is he like! A complete arse! Was he trying to be a swinger again?"

"He was when I went in."

"Listen, let me tell you, if it's not golf it's those punishment lines, women in rubber knickers telling him what a naughty boy he is and giving him a cyber smack. He doesn't realise what a wasted resource *I* am. If he paid me what he spends on the Internet I'd give him a ten minute belting every morning. No problem"

"He might get all excited and make demands on you, Patsy."

"It would be the last demand he ever made! I'm fussy; no' foosty."

"Talking of which, Mrs Somner's been waiting about ten minutes now, I'd better go in to see her."

"OK. A call came in for you from a Mrs Lawrence. She said it was private and left a number to call her back."

Carol took the note with the phone number, although she knew her aunt's number by heart.

"Thanks, I'll get round to it."

Her next meeting, with Mrs Somner, was less fun - a part-time office worker, of middle years, smartly dressed, with a gold chain round her neck, at the end of which was a pair of spectacles with lenses like milk bottle bottoms. She'd need to keep out of direct sunlight or she'd set her boobs on fire. Probably shouldn't even be driving. She was lucky the Police never booked her, never mind her suing them for damages. Carol's job was to give out measured advice however, not to speak her mind.

"I see here Mrs Somner that you were offered £800 to settle out of court."

"Yes, Mr Ogilvie agreed with me it was quite an insult."

Carol could feel the hot breath of the Law Society on Gavin's neck.

"It would have paid for the repairs to the front of the car, and made up for your loss of 'No Claims' Bonus."

"Well, yes, but there's a principle at stake. I was very shaken, you know."

"I appreciate that, but I'm wondering if it would be wise to accept the offer, even at this late stage. Sheriff Court decisions can go either way you know."

"No, Miss Reid, I've made my mind up about this. If you are unsure, can't Mr Ogilvie deal with this?"

"I'm afraid he's engaged tomorrow, and all this week."

"What a pity."

Gavin was flying over to California, to a golf tournament. She wondered what this old bat would say if she knew her precious Mr Ogilvie had dropped her at the last minute to go on a jaunt.

"Yes, he's going to be involved in negotiations with some of our U.S. colleagues."

Mrs Somner looked impressed. "Oh, my, he's come very far for such a young man."

"Yes, he's very well disciplined."

But only from 18.39 hrs until 19.01 hrs, according to his Internet history. Sometimes Patsy just didn't have enough to keep her occupied.

"In fact, Mrs Somner, I wouldn't be surprised if he was just as, if not more disciplined, when he goes on his trans-continental mission."

There were bound to be a selection of smack and whack clubs in the Sunshine State.

Mrs Somner looked at her as if she was some idiot child.

"Anyway, Mrs Somner, I'm afraid you'll be stuck with me tomorrow. For your sins."

"Glasgow Sheriff Court, 10am. Please be prompt, Miss Reid. Now, do you know where it is?"

Once she finally left, Carol buzzed through to Patsy.

"Patsy, me darlin', have you any Halloween

cakes left?"

In the afternoon Carol looked out the slip of paper she'd been given in the morning. Mrs Lawrence. Auntie Sarah. Robert's mother. To anyone outside the family, it would seem such a simple case: he'd insulted a pub full of Orangemen, one had chased after him, found him, beaten him and killed him, possibly accidentally. But absolutely *nobody* in Brigton was helping the Police with their enquiries. Yet Robert was a local boy, and Dan and Sarah were respected members of the Orange Order, surely there couldn't be a cover up?

The phone was answered after two rings.

"Hello."

"Auntie Sarah. It's Carol here ..."

"Carol, I hope you didnae mind me calling you during the day. Your mammy's no' in much these days, and I tried to get your home number from your daddy but he isnae at himself ..."

Carol's dad, Archie. Four months of phone calls to Social Workers and he was still no nearer to getting into a home. 'Supported living in the community', which meant pishing himself twice a day, refusing to answer the door to his home help and nurse, and Carol's mother on the verge of a breakdown.

"Don't worry, you're fine. What can I do for you, Auntie Sarah?"

Carol was worried. Had Sarah found out about Josie? Carol had never told a soul about their meeting. Over the weeks, she'd been trying to persuade Josie to meet Sarah, but she'd been taking it easy, in fear of pressuring the girl, in case it made her more determined to stay hidden.

"Start calling me Sarah, for a start. You're making me feel old."

"Sorry. Right then – Sarah."

"I just thought you might want to come up for your tea. You could tell me how you're getting on."

"OK. When?"

"After your work tomorrow? Dan'll be out at the bowling, so we can have a wee talk in peace."

Carol arranged to visit Sarah at six o'clock the next evening. Then concentrated on her final two calls.

The first call was to Josie.

"Josie. Hi, it's Carol."

"Carol, how're you doing? Do you know, I'm having Jim up here for his lunch, and he keeps asking about you ..."

"That's funny. I had someone on the phone just now, who, I think, was asking about **you**."

"Who? The guy from the Lottery I hope."

"My Aunt Sarah."

"Oh."

The line went silent for a moment.

"What did she want?"

"You. She wants me to go up for my tea tomorrow, no doubt to see if I've found you yet. I'm sure of it."

"Well, tell her you never managed to trace me."

"You don't know the women in my family. They're relentless. She'll find you anyway. It's only a matter of time."

"And when she does, she'll be getting short shrift from me."

"Well, it's your decision, Josie."

"It is indeed. Anyway, what about my big brother? He's trying to act cool, but he's starting to crack. Are you interested or not?"

Carol wasn't sure. She'd only ever met him once. But then again, she was in danger of becoming a born-again virgin.

"Are you still there, Carol?"

"Me and Patsy are going to the Halloween Quiz Night tonight in 'The Spuig'. About nine. I might see him in there?"

"*Verree* interesting. I'll let him know. And I'll see you later in the week then?"

"Yes, I'll pop by."

"What night?"

"Thursday. I'll come up about eight."

"Great. I'll get a bottle of wine and watch you get drunk."

"Make it white. Red wine turns my lips purple. Bye for now."

"Bye, Carol".

The second call was to her father's Social Worker. Carol usually kept her private life away from her professional life but Sarah's call had reminded her that a call to Peter Watson was overdue.

She phoned the Social Work office and asked for him, without saying who she was. For a change, she was put through immediately.

The voice was smooth and confident.

"Hi, Peter Watson here. Senior Social Worker"

"Hello Peter. Carol Reid here. Nice to hear you've been promoted."

A slight pause.

"Ah Carol. Good to hear from you. I take it you're phoning about Archie?"

"None other."

"No movement on the waiting list, I'm afraid."

"Have you phoned the home this week?"

"Well no, but ..."

"Have you spoken to my father at all in the last few weeks?"

"Carol, my caseload doesn't allow me a lot of home visits, except in emergency cases ..."

"The Council were out last week fumigating his house; he's soiled it so many times."

"But his home help and nurse should be helping him out with that."

"He's too senile to open the door to them. He thinks they're trying to rob him. Have you had any word from his doctor?"

"Yes!" Peter sounded relieved to be able to answer in the affirmative.

"Yes, indeed, I'm just getting your father's file out now. Yes, here it is; a letter from his GP at Bridgeton Health Centre. Let me see, blah blah blah, no there's nothing helpful here I'm afraid."

Carol wasn't getting fobbed off with this crap.

"So the doctor actually wrote 'blah, blah, blah'? Is that a medical term, Peter?"

"No, of course, he didn't actually ..."

"Well, what does the letter say?"

She heard the rustle of paper against the phone.

"Mr Reid is confused and has a defective short term memory. In addition, he has emphysema and is also suffering from osteoarthritis in his left arm and leg. His mental state is a result, in my opinion, of years of alcohol misuse and is therefore untreatable. He is a heavy smoker, which is the greatest causative factor of emphysema. Mr Reid is still capable of living at home, or with a member of his family, if he is given appropriate support. As to his arthritis, I have referred him to the Physiotherapy Department at Glasgow Royal Infirmary on several occasions, all of which he has failed to attend."

You have to admit Carol, it's not looking good."

"In what way?"

"Homes don't like to take alcoholics, in case they cause disruptions."

"He *was* an alcoholic. He's too old to drink now."

"The doctor mentions a member of the family. What about you or your mother ..."

"Under no circumstances, Peter. My mum's been *divorced* from him for four years, for Christ's sake. She shouldn't be looking after him at all, but she goes up every second day to wash him down. She's getting too old for that."

"You're a young woman ..."

"With a full-time job! Don't even think about it."

She was determined that Peter was not going to lay some guilt-trip on her, make her out to be the ungrateful child throwing her father on the scrap heap when he got too old to be useful. Archie wasn't coming to stay with her, and that was that. Annie was allowed to divorce him because he was a bad husband. Weren't children allowed to divorce bad parents?

"All I'm saying Carol, is that it doesn't look good, if even his own family will have nothing to do with him ..."

"Look Peter, I go up there every Saturday to help my mother out. We have to look after him because your care in the community, like most theoretical constructs, has collapsed round about us."

"He's got a nurse and a home help."

"So you've said. It's a matter of record that he won't answer the door. He's frightened to open it, for Christ's sake."

"That's the other thing, Carol. He'd been holding drinking parties. The neighbours complained to the Housing Department."

'Drinking parties'! Bloody Hell, was this guy the full shilling?

"Listen Peter, because he is *senile*, he let men into his house, and these men took advantage of a *senile* old man and used his house as a drinking den. They took all his pension money, and his army pension."

"He signed the pensions over to them himself. We had the signatures checked."

"So what you're telling me, Peter, is that because his condition is largely his own fault, and because his lifestyle leaves a lot to be desired, you will not help him?"

"*Will not* is putting it rather strongly Carol, it's just that there are more deserving cases out there …"

"Peter, if we all lived a wholesome, good-citizen type of life you would be redundant. You're a bloody Social Worker! You're *paid* to care for the *undeserving*! That's your bloody job!"

"Now Carol, this is not helpful …"

She hung up. He was right, she wasn't very helpful, but an arse like Peter should have been used to insults. She put her face on the cool wood of her desk, closed her eyes and sighed. Life was getting far too complicated.

Chapter Six

Tomorrow was his day off. Today was Frew's. Forty-eight hours without having to clock the miserable bastard's ugly mug. It was Halloween tonight. Frew could go out as himself and still terrify all the weans.

Wee Mags was at it again. She'd nipped out the back for a fag half an hour ago. Still, at least when she was out there she wisnae torturing him with her change of life stories. He might be a butcher, but he couldnae cope with all the blood and gore. Heart, kidneys, lungs, legs, wings. Cows, sheep, chickens and sometimes rabbits - he could cope with *them*, could skin, bone, slice, dress. But he didnae want to hear about, never mind fuckin' *talk* about, ovaries, sweats, cramps, or, in the name of fuck, 'it all coming away' from her. What did that mean? No, don't go there. Don't even think about asking.

How could Mags not be like his ma – when he was wee and one of her pals hinted at the dreaded 'troubles', him and Michael were given a sweetie and told to play outside, while his ma and the other women got down to the finer details.

The place was dead. To give himself something to do he fronted the shelves. To add more excitement to his day, he looked out the window. The rain was keeping all the women indoors. The pensioner with the string message bag would be in for her meat parcel soon though. He didnae know her name. She always came in on a Tuesday afternoon, always got Jim to serve her. Mags thought the old dear had a wee thing for him. What she didnae know was that he'd been undercharging her ever since he clocked her swiping a packet of tattie scones when she thought he was in the back shop. She had a nice face, kind, the way his ma would have looked if she'd lived to be a pensioner. A lady.

He told himself she was lifting stuff because she'd a man who didnae give her enough house-keeping but knocked her about if he didnae get three square meals. That's how she took the scones, although she shifted them at some speed, practically sleight of hand. Still, he didnae want her lifted and it was Frew's profits.

Here she was now: see through plastic rain-mate thing on her head; ancient coat, probably posh in its day; string bag. Mags didnae like serving her anyway, said she used to take men in when she was young, the talk of the street at one time. There were letters to the factor but nothing had been done about it. But that was just Mags' hormones, getting a decent old dear mixed up with some wee strumpet from years ago.

"Whit a day son!" she took her rain mate off and gave it a good shake, splattering rain over the glass fronted counter. Good job Wee Mags was on the skive.

"You're drookit, missus!"

"I know son, but you'd go off your heid stuck in thae flats all day. And forbye that, if you don't get oot you stiffen up."

"Quite right, missus. Is it your usual order?"

"Aye, son."

Four pork loin chops. A pound of Pope's Eye steak. Two pounds of mince, in four half pound bags. A pound of pork links and three square sausages. A packet of puff pastry and twelve stock cubes. Two chicken breasts and two thighs. Three quarters of tongue and a half pound of gammon. All this for one wee woman – she'd get scurvy if she didnae watch it.

"Right missus, that comes to ten pounds and eighty-five pence."

"Are you sure son? It was only ten pounds sixty last week."

He couldnae mind what he charged last week. That was the problem with just making it up.

"Your chops are big today missus."

"Aw right son. It just seemed awfy dear, but."

Most of the time, he couldnae be doing with customers that moaned about prices. But she was smiling at him, not like the usual bunch with their girning coupons.

"Whit aboot a wee ham hough flung in? For your soup? And a bag of peanuts for the weans the night?"

"Oh, I don't make soup son. Too many vegetables to cut up. An' I don't open my doors at night son. No' even to the weans with their guises. There's that many fly folk oot there."

Wee Mags started the cleaning up early, she had to get home and get elevated as soon as possible. Swollen legs. It suited him to be finished sharp, he was off to the Fancy Dress Quiz Night in 'The Spuig'.

When he'd went up to see Josie in his dinner break, he'd found her all excited about Carol, who apparently had dropped a heavy hint that she'd like to see him tonight. Carol would be a bit of a catch. Nice looking, kind, good personality and all that stuff that's supposed to be important, and probably into world peace. And, he had to admit, a fine pair of tits. He kept trying not to stare, but they were *so* fine. Not big droopy ones, like Wee Mags, and not the tiny ones that made him feel awkward, like he was shagging a boy. Not that he'd shagged anybody in about nine months. He'd balls like melons to prove it.

Carol's breasts looked like a good handful a piece, but he doubted if he'd ever get to try them out. She was a lawyer, good salary, mortgage, all that stuff. What would she see in him? It was better not to get his hopes up. Or any other part of his anatomy, for that matter.

By half past five, Mags had cleaned the fridges and the trays, mopped the floor, washed and dried the cold meat and bacon slicers. Polished the glass counters. He'd put the stock away in the back fridge, cashed up the till, put the takings in the safe and got the float ready for the morning.

As they were on their way out the door, he told Mags he'd left his scarf in the back shop, and she was just to get up the road with her legs, he'd lock up by himself.

When he came back out, he had a scarf wrapped round his neck and leather jacket buttoned up as far as it would go. Right, into 'The Spuig' for a quick one and then up the road to get washed and changed.

It was only six o'clock but the bar was heaving. Since they built the new flats there was a right mix of customers – guys in working overalls and guys in suits – all just out of their work. But the funny thing was, the working guys wore suits to get brammed up and the suits kicked about in casual gear when they were out on the sniff. The quiz teams were mixed, but. They were wee classless societies. It didnae matter whether you were in overalls or a suit, as long as you knew the answers. He'd often thought that was where the Soviets had got it wrong - too many labour camps, not enough Quiz Nights.

He made his way to the front of the crowd at the bar, tenner in his hand. He should just get his tea here. There'd be no seats later. Siobhan came up to serve him. Jesus lumpen fuck, another fine woman! Plenty to get hold of, in all the right places, an arse just made for you to bite. Not that he would dare – he'd seen what happened to a guy who tried it. He didnae know how strong a female could be until that moment. She'd lifted the arsehole up by his collar, put an arm lock on him and then ran him out the door, using his face to open it. She took a couple of seconds to get her breath, and then went straight back to clearing glasses.

"Jim, what can I get you?"

She smiled at him, looked pleased to see him. Big brown eyes, lovely long hair and high cheekbones. Dressed for the party night like an Indian squaw. Her skirt reached her ankles, but when she moved in front of the bottle cabinet you could see her long, strong but ever so womanly thighs against the light. You could open a beer bottle on those thighs. How could she and Wee Mags even live on the same planet?

"Pint of Guinness, please. What have you got for eating?"

"I've only got cheese and tomato rolls left. We've been cleared out by all these boys here."

"Did you make them yourself, doll?"

Siobhan's wide beaming smile shrank a wee bit.

"Yes."

She thought he was gonnae start the patter, and she was right. Although what could he say that she'd not heard a million times before? She was too scary for him anyway. Dangerous, as well. If he got lucky with Siobhan he'd have a different guy digging him up every time he came in here. Jealousy was a terrible thing.

"Give us two rolls then. And a bag of salt and vinegar."

She tilted a pint glass under the Guinness tap, until the foam reached the top and then put it aside to settle, then she laid the food and crisps on the counter, and folded up a napkin for him. There were good vibes from her again, now that he'd backed off.

"Jim, are you not boiling with that scarf on, and your jacket all done up? We've got the heating on, you know!"

"I was working a lot in the freezers the day, and I huvenae thawed out yet."

"Oh, well, it's up to you. Have a seat and I'll bring your Guinness over when it's ready."

He took his food and went over to Eddie's table. He'd been pally with him ever since they were at school.

"How you doin' Ed? Got a pass fae Angela?"

"That's more than you'll be getting' fae the Siobhan yin."

Jim sat down, bracing himself for the pelters to come.

"I was watchin' you chancing it, you fuckin' toerag? You've nae chance there, Jimbo!"

"How do *you* know? Tried it yoursel, like?"

"Hey, I've got all I need waitin' for me back home."

That was true, Angela was yet *another* fine woman that was out of his reach. Jim had fancied her at school: it wisnae just sad old geezers who

71

got excited about teenage girls in school uniforms. Angela had caused him to wake up stuck to his sheets many a time, but Eddie had nipped in there and that was that. Even though Jim had tellt him how he liked her. Trusted him, the bastard. He never tellt him about the sheets though.

"I'm an impartial observer, just like thae UN cunts. I just watch and laugh. She'll never get aff with a punter in here. You're aw in a Catch 22: she's no' the type to go chasin' men but if you show you're interested she freezes you oot."

"Maybe she likes women better."

"That's whit you rejected cunts aw say: "Ah'm that pure gemme, that if she doesnae want to shag me, she's a dyke!""

Sometimes Eddie was a smug bastard. He'd go too far one day.

"Would you fuckin' listen to yoursel' Eddie! Are you some kinda new man? Dead sensitive an' aw that? Or has Angela been puttin' her birth pills in your tea?"

"The lassie just doesnae go oot with punters, that's all. Anyway, whit's with the scarf an' the jaicket? You're sweatin' like a rapist. You got pleurisy or somethin'?"

"Somethin'. Feeling a bit rough, so I'm wrapping up warm."

"Ya big girl's blouse!"

"If only!" said Jim, thinking of Carol.

"Aye, pardon the pun. But you'll start hyperventilatin' with aw that gear on."

"Naw I'll no! I'm cool, awright?"

He wisnae but. He was cooking. When Siobhan came over with his pint he drank it in half a dozen gulps and ordered another round for him and Eddie. Followed by another, and another. Somehow he never made it home, and then it was too late, folk all coming in for the quiz. Three other guys and two lassies came to join his table, to make up a team for the quiz. He peered at his female quiz mates through an alcohol haze. It was that wee blonde – Patsy? And Carol, yes, Carol! She was sitting beside him.

Eddie was voted captain. How did that chancer always get to be captain? "Gorbals Diehards" their team was called. No' very original but there you go. By the time the quiz started he was half steaming but he only loosened his scarf a bit. When he went for a slash he told anybody that asked that he'd tonsillitis.

The prize tonight was a case of lager. There were seven in the team so there wouldnae be an even split. Sanferryan to him - he didnae like lager. How come the other teams were dressed funny? One lot had thae Baldy Bain wigs on, with big bits of hair sticking out the side, ready to take your eyeballs out if they moved too fast. Big Groucho Marx 'taches. The other lot were just guys in suits and the last lot were clad head to foot in Glasgow Rangers strips. Cunts. Then he remembered that he'd forgot. It was fancy dress. He could tell folk he'd come as a tomato.

He was more worried that he felt like he was listening to Radio Luxembourg: one minute he could hear everything, the next minute everybody was talking interference. Another effect of being blootered was that by the time they got to the last round he had a ten second delay between hearing a question and answering it.

QUIZ MASTER	Finnair is what country's airline?
JIM	Sassinfrazzinrassin.
QUIZ MASTER	In which month is St. Andrew's Day?
JIM	I know that one! Finland.
QUIZ MASTER:	What type of animal is an ibex?
JIM	They questions are fuckin' easy. Sorry ladies! November. Eddie, you writin' this down?
QUIZ MASTER	In which country is Dalaman Airport?
JIM	I think it's a goat. Or a big cat. One of the two. What youse laughin' at?
QUIZ MASTER	What is the traditional female dress for Scottish country dancing?

JIM	It's one of those places you go your holidays. What is it again – Turkey! Oh here, that prize's got oor name on it! Nae tother a' baw!
QUIZ MASTER	OK, ladies and gents. If you want to hand your papers in we'll get the final score. A wee reminder of the scores so far: Gorbals Die-hards and the South Side True Blues are neck and neck with 42 points, Cumbie Thirty - Some - thing's are on 36. The Einstein-A-Go-Go's are trailing on 25.
JIM	Fucked if I know. Basque and sussies? Naw it's a bit cold in Teuchterland for that sort of thing.
QUIZ MASTER	While the lovely Kylie is tallying up the final scores I'll go over the answers to the last round ques-tions. They were: Finland, Nov-ember, a goat, Turkey, and a tartan dress with a sash. I'm sure the South Side True Blues got that last one. Get it? Sash? Eh? Only kidding gents! We're ready to give you the final tally now: Einstein-A-Go-Go are now on 28

– bad luck chaps – change the name eh, tempting fate there. Cumbie Thirty Some - thing's haven't moved at 38. South Side True Blues are on 46 but the winners tonight with a score of 47 and a prize of a case of lager are: the Gorbals Die-hards.

JIM   Whit happened? Did we win? I knew it! EASSSY!

Ladies, seen as youse are so nice youse can have my share. I don't really drink you know, and I really need to get home. Watch that Eddie. He's a fly bastard. Language, language, sorry, sorry. Carol, see you, you're lovely. An' you're a lovely person, helping oot Josie. An' a really don't mind that you're some kinda posh burd – have you ever considered getting married? Oh, for fuck's sake, don't answer that, I'm steamin' and talkin' pish. Right, keys up, I'm away. Cheerio. Mind, you know where to find me if you're lookin' – Tuesdays. PM. Cheap meat afternoon.

Jim squeezed through the crowds. He had to get outside before he threw up. He was crumpled, greasy, smelling like an old hoor's hankie. When he got out, the chill air slapped him sober. He wished he hadnae gibbered shite to Carol.

It was a few hours since his last lot of scoff and now he had the munchies. It was too late to start making dinners. He fancied a fish supper. And a big bottle of something fizzy. He couldnae wake up with a hangover, he'd a busy day ahead of him tomorrow. There were a few of the top guys in Paisley waiting for him to deliver. He was late last time: just didnae have enough to give them. If he let them down again he knew he'd be on his way out.

The chippie was only a hundred yards away from the pub, past the high flats. He could see these wee figures in the background, pirates and ghosties. Only wee weans but they were spooky, the way they ran from one block of flats to the other, never making a sound, disappearing in the darkness and then reappearing and caught in the lights from the concierge's office. He shivered but it could have been the high wind caused by the tall buildings, it nearly knocked him off his feet. It was freezing, as well. Good job he was well wrapped up, although he felt his nose starting to run.

He was about twenty yards from the chippie when he saw a kerfuffle. A gang fight, by the looks of it. His first reaction was to veer away to the left, go home, make do with a piece on fried egg and a cup of tea. Let them batter the fuck out of each other. Not his problem.

But there was something up, something not right. It was too quiet for a gang fight, not enough shouts of bravado, of come ahead ya bams, and stuff like that. He went closer. There were four of them, kicking into one solitary figure on the ground, who was rolled into a ball, offering no resistance. The only noise was the fut-fut of boots on flesh. Jim hesitated: if he just breenged in, he'd be next. The guy on the ground wisnae too handy or he wouldnae be in the state he was in.

He couldnae leave it. The guy on the ground had just given up. Game's a bogey. But they wouldnae quit. This silent kicking was gonnae go on 'til he was dead. This wisnae just scary or spooky, this was real life.

Jim prepared himself. He looked around for weapons. There was a big bit of metal tube lying out on the road nearby, remnants of a bus stop or something. He ran over, grabbed it, and took a deep breath.

He breenged in.

The element of surprise was on his side. He caught one of them a crack on the head and he fell to the ground, clutching his bleeding wound. Jim dealt him a swift kick to the balls. To make sure he stayed down. The other three were aiming feet and fists at his body, but couldnae get near enough for the tube he was swinging.

"C'MON THEN, PRICKS!"

He was taunting them, trying to out-psyche them. He beckoned them with the bent fingers of one hand, the other still wrapped round his weapon. The adrenaline was pumping through his body. He was gonnae have these bastards, no bother.

They all reached inside their jackets at the same time. He should've known they'd be tooled up.

The tall one lunged at him. The knife slashed the air, missing him by the skin of his scrotum. The force of the lunge caused the guy to keep going and he staggered right in front of him. Jim grabbed the hair at the top of his head and smashed the guy's face down onto his knee. He heard the click of a breaking nose. Jim's trouser legs were splattered in blood: he skelped the back of the fucker's skull with the tube and dropped him to the ground. This one was going nowhere.

Another landed a kick to his thigh. He never felt a thing, but it flung him off balance. On the way down he swiped at the cunt's shins. Heard a crack. Another one down. Jim rolled over and was up on his feet in an instant. The one he'd hobbled on the way down was crawling away. Just in case he made a comeback, Jim dealt him a swift boot to the kidneys and he arced in the air with pain.

He looked round for the guy he was trying to rescue. Glaikit cunt. He was sitting up, watching, mouth hanging open. Could he not sort himself out and lend a hand?

This second of broken concentration was all it

took. He saw a knife, saw it disappear into his chest up to the hilt.

What happened next could have lasted five seconds or five hours. He staggered onto the street and collapsed to his knees. A car was coming towards him. It screeched to a stop a few yards away. He saw three sets of legs get in. Somebody else was getting carried. He heard the engine being revved and the car wheels spin. They were coming for him to finish him off. No fucking way! He flung himself into the gutter just as the car sped past, stotting his head off the kerb. He only just made it but the car had caught his jacket, bursting open the buttons. The car's reverse lights came on. Then he heard voices. Men and women were running towards him. The reverse lights went off and the car disappeared up the road.

Then there was a crowd round him, moving him onto the pavement. Even the useless shite he'd saved from being kicked to death had stirred himself.

"No way man, that blade was meant for me. Whit a hero, man. Stay still. There's an ambulance coming. You're the main man, man."

What was he on about? Was he some kind of American?

There were other voices round him.

"Get the knife out of him!"

"No don't! It's staunching the bleeding. I saw it in *Casualty*!"

"Loosen his clothing then, help him to breathe."

He tried to stop them touching him, but he was wasted from the dunt on the head. He had trouble breathing, and a terrible pain in his chest. His jacket had burst open anyway, it was only the knife holding it in place. Someone unbuttoned his shirt, and that's when it happened. Women screaming. One of them fainting on the spot, a big lassie too, dressed as a French Maid. She would've broken his ribs if she'd landed on him. There was a reason for that but he'd forgotten again.

Only his ribs were already broken. That was the pain. One of them was sticking out through his shirt.

He managed to sit up. There was more screaming, not all female.

"Mother of God, they've ripped him apart!"

"But he's still alive! Look at him, he's moving his head!"

"That's what happens to chickens. Doesnae mean they're no' deid!"

"Maybe he's done up as somebody for his Halloween. Queer fuckin' get-up mind you."

He'd had enough of these crazies. He was getting out of there. As he stood up, his ribs fell to the ground, exposing what was underneath. He felt freezing cold, but suddenly a lot lighter.

If it wisnae for his tee shirt he'd be getting pneumonia by now. He wisnae sure if this was the right time or place but he sent up a wee prayer anyway, to the patron saint of butchers, to thank him for helping him to liberate the two sides of ham ribs out the back shop all those hours ago. Some poor pig perished that he might live.

Still, if he ever tried that trick again he was going straight home after work. With them stuck up under his shirt the heat had nearly done for him and they'd been pure murder to carry about in the pub. With his jacket done up and his scarf he must have looked wired to the moon.

He picked up his ribs, flicking off bits of grit. He wrapped them in what was left of his jacket. They'd need a good rinse before he boiled them up for soup. He'd have no bother breaking them up, they were half smashed with all the stramash. Hey, was that a poem? "The poet that didnae know it." The knife was still embedded in one of the sides of ribs. Come in handy for cutting up the vegetables for his soup. At least he knew it was sharp enough.

Without a word to the folk round about, he buttoned his shirt and walked off into the night.

Chapter Seven

Carol felt her heart sink as Sarah left the room. Her aunt had made ham and tomato sandwiches, with home-made cake to follow. Cups and saucers, milk jug and sugar bowl. Old fashioned china, a wedding gift, silver spoons, and cloth napkins. When she was a wee girl, Sarah would give her a cup of tea in a mug and her dinner on a tea tray on her knee.

It was a dreich November night and Carol could see her breath before her as Sarah had shown her into the front room. Sarah had put the double bars on the electric fire: the dusty smell coming from it reminded her that this was the 'good' room, only for special visitors.

Sarah came back carrying a silver tea pot, which she placed on a lace doily, beside the rest of the spread.

"Carol, pet, thanks for coming down. I know you're busy."

It was the second time in two days that Carol had been called pet. But this was going to be a much trickier conversation than with old ma Somner. The same old ma Somner - whose petition had been flung out by the Sheriff that very morning, as Carol had so confidently predicted.

Carol looked around the room, stalling for time.

"That's a fine picture on the wall there."

"Which one, the Queen's?"

Queen Elizabeth the Second was framed above the fireplace. She looked to be in her thirties, and was wearing some kind of ball gown and orange sash. Carol had actually meant the copy of Rembrandt's Laughing Cavalier on the other wall.

"Yes. A hard working woman, Her Majesty," she said.

"The best of the lot. Mind you, I was going to shift her to the dining recess and put Robert's graduation photo there. She'll be staying where she is now."

Carol knew what was coming next, but she still couldn't bring herself to get to the subject in hand.

"I'm really sorry about what happened to him, Sarah. We hardly saw each other, over the last wee while. We had a lot of laughs when he was a wee boy. Do you remember that New Year?"

"When he came and played the accordion and your daddy was trying to give him ten shillings to play The Sash?"

"That's right, but he never played it, 'cos Mrs Quinn was in."

"Aye, and she's still living yet, although she's an old, old wumman now."

"She hated her man, remember, and nobody knew 'till he died?"

"That's right, the diabetes finally killed him, that and the toffee she was aye making for him. Not a tooth in his head when he passed away. Mind you, he was cruel to her, we could hear him shouting the odds when he had a drink in him. Robbie never liked him. When he was a wee baby he'd start greetin' whenever he saw the dour big beggar."

Sarah looked over Carol's shoulder, a faint smile on her lips. Then she seemed to make a conscious effort to draw herself back to the present day.

"Onyway, Carol, let's talk about Robbie's girlfriend."

The directness of this statement surprised Carol. Did Sarah know about Josie's baby? Did she know of Carol's friendship with her? How could that be? Carol had made a point of not even telling her own mother.

"I just know in my heart that she's a Catholic. That must be how he never tellt us about her. He thought we'd go against her."

"Would you have?"

"Robbie was a good boy but he was thrawn. Nae doubt he was fond of the lassie, but the added attraction would have been her no' being one of us."

"So he never joined the Lodge, then?"

"He wanted to when he was a wee boy. You'll mind him carrying the banner on the children's parade? No, well, he did, just the once, but when he got that bit older he got awkward. He said we were bigots, when we were just trying to protect him frae Roman Catholicism."

"Sarah, do you really think in this day and age

a grown man like Robert needed protected from Catholics?"

"Not frae Catholics. This is where them outside the Order get it wrong. We've got nothing against Catholics, as long as they don't impose their religion on us. It's the brainwashing that goes with the religion we're against. *That's* what we're trying to protect the young ones from."

"And are Orangemen and Protestants not brainwashed?"

"How can we be? Think about the name – *Protest*ants – protesting against idolatry and the worship of things made oot of plaster and wood. And Popes. Oor *consciences* guide us as to how we worship God and live up to Christ's message. Not some old Italian thoosan's of miles away, dictating how you should *think*, never mind live."

Carol had heard this all before, from Archie, her dad.

"The Pope's German."

"He could be a Martian, for all he matters to God."

Archie never made references to God and Christ as Sarah did. Carol had always suspected that her dad never really believed in anything, it was just that he wanted to feel better than somebody else, in this case Catholics. He was white trash without the trailer park or the Elvis statuettes.

Sarah was holding a cup and saucer in one hand, teapot in the other. Expertly, she poured tea directly from the pot into the cup, without spilling a drop. With a steady hand, she offered the drink to Carol, and then took a deep breath.

"You maybe think yourself that I'm some religious fanatic, Carol, but it's just what I believe. I don't hate onybody for being a Catholic, I feel sorry for them, more than onything".

This was the first real adult conversation Carol had ever had with Sarah, but this woman seemed made of sterner stuff than her dad. Maybe she really was a believer. But Sarah's attitude bothered Carol. All the circumstances pointed to a man from Brigton having murdered Robert, someone who had been celebrating the Orange Walk and who took offence at whatever Robert had shouted in that pub. How could his mother still feel a part of that world?

As if following her train of thoughts, Sarah looked directly at Carol.

"I just cannae believe it was somebody frae Brigton that attacked him. It just doesnae make ony sense."

"Why not?"

"If it was somebody local we'd have been tellt who he was by now."

"Someone could be hiding him."

"Brigton's no' big enough to hide this fella."

"So where d'you think he's hiding?"

"I huvnae a clue, pet. All I'm sure of is that I need to find out more about my boy. Especially where he lived his life."

"I thought he still lived at home?"

"That's where he kept his clothes."

Carol was silent while she thought of the implications of this statement. It was Sarah who spoke first.

"This lassie must know something I don't. I'm desperate to speak to her."

This story didn't tie in with Josie's.

"What would you have done if Robert had brought home this Catholic girl?"

"As I said, Carol, we're not bigots. We'd have made her welcome."

"Have you never met her, then?"

"Do you think if I knew her I'd be looking for her now?"

According to Josie she was shunned at Robert's funeral, yet Sarah seemed to be genuinely telling the truth.

Carol looked at her cup. The tea was starting to cool. She reached for a teaspoon, and kept stirring, so that she would not have to look Sarah in the eye.

"Don't you think it's strange she never went to the funeral?"

"The only young folk at the funeral were some boys' frae the University and Michael ..."

Sarah never finished the sentence.

"Carol, are you trying to tell me something? I'll find out one way or another, mind."

Carol was sure of that.

"Her name is Josie. She's due to have your

grandchild about February."

"She's *expecting*!"

Sarah clattered the teapot onto the table, missing the lace doily completely. There would be heat stains on the wood.

"How do you know all this?"

"I met her by sheer chance."

"And you never thought to let us know?"

Sarah sounded more hurt and disappointed than angry, which made Carol feel about ten years old.

"She didn't want anything to do with you. She said she tried to talk to you at the funeral but you ignored her. She was with Michael."

"With Michael?"

"He's her cousin."

Sarah was looking over Carol's shoulder again, rerunning Robert's funeral.

"In the name of goodness! I get the picture now. I thought she was Michael's girlfriend. I was just too upset to speak, that's all. They should have forced me to listen."

"Looks like both sides got the wrong impression."

There was a long silence, both women lost in their thoughts. She wasn't sure what Sarah was thinking, but Carol was worrying how she was going to break it to Josie that she'd done the one thing she'd promised not to.

Again Sarah was first to talk.

"I need to speak to her, make it up to her. Does

she live with her family now?"

"I don't think she's got much family. Only a brother and Michael."

"What about her mammy and daddy?"

"Her mother's dead and her father's disowned her."

"So you must know where she lives."

This was a statement from Sarah, not a question. Carol decided to draw some willpower back from wherever it had disappeared to.

"I do."

"So tell me."

"I must speak to Josie first. If you think about it, that would be the best thing to do. I can explain the mix up at the funeral. I promise I will tell you how to contact her once I have spoken to her."

Carol made a conscious decision to only promise to tell Sarah how to contact Josie, not to give out the girl's address. Sarah thought about this for a few seconds, nodded acceptance.

"Fair enough. But don't take too long, or I'll chap every door in the Gorbals 'til I find her."

Carol had to get home, to work out a plan. She reached for her coat, which was warming by the fire. As Sarah helped her into it, she sighed.

"Your daddy's not very well, Carol."

"He should be in a home, but it's not that easy."

"In my day we looked after old folk ourselves."

Sarah saw the look on Carol's face.

"Mind you, it was a terrible strain on the women, they had to do all the cleaning up after them, as well as look after their men and their weans."

"Times have changed, Sarah."

"I know, pet. I quite understand."

"It's the worry that the Tam one will come back. Dad's too far gone to keep him out."

"Have you reported him to the Polis?"

"Yes, but there's nothing they can do, unless they catch him in the house, and even then they can only throw him out. They can't stop him coming back, 'cos at the moment he's doing nothing illegal. Dad opens the door to him and lets him in."

"I'll speak to Dan about Archie. Maybe the Lodge can sort something out."

"Like what?"

"I don't really know. I'll leave it up to the men folk."

Carol put her coat on over her jacket. She didn't want to know how the men folk would sort it out.

* * *

It was Carol's birthday. Ten today. Daddy was taking her and her wee cousin, Robert, to the pictures. James Bond. 007. They had to go on the bus as it was far away. Mammy was at her work.

There was a big queue. Daddy wanted to come back tomorrow but Carol started crying. The queue might be bigger tomorrow. This might be the last chance to see the film before it went back to America!

There was a pub up the road from the picture house.

Daddy was going to nip in 'til the queue died down. He'd bring out coke and crisps for her and Robert. He was away a long time. When he came out, he had a carrier bag with four cans in it - a wee drink for in the picture house. Carol was to look after it. He forgot the coke and crisps so he went back in for them.

Two boys came up to them. The wee one spat on Robert. He just started crying – he never stuck up for himself, even though he was bigger than the boy. Carol told them to beat it – their daddy was coming out and he'd get them. The big one went right up to Carol and stuck his face right against hers. His mouth was twisted and he'd lots of slabbers in it. How could he hate her when he didn't know her? She was to give him the bag and they'd go away. It was her daddy's stuff: if she gave it to him she'd get belted.

The wee one kicked Robert in the stomach. 'You want the bag? Here, take it!' She swung it round over her head, her arm straight out. The bag landed right in the middle of the big one's head. 'You've burst ma heid open, ya cow!' He'd his hands over his head. She couldn't see any blood but her arm was sore. The wee one and Robert were staring at her.

'Whit's goin' on here!' Daddy came out of the pub. She started crying again – she wanted to go home. 'She's burst ma heid open!' Daddy looked at her: 'Whit did you do that for?' He put his hand up, but Robert jumped in front of her. 'He was goin' to steal your cans, Uncle Archie!' She was looking at her daddy's arm, waiting for the slap. He put his hand down. 'That's right, daddy. Can we go now?' Her daddy looked at the

92

boy. He was crying on the ground. The other one had run away. 'Let's get out of here. Place is full of bampots.'

Chapter Eight

"**S**o you told her."

This was from Josie, about three seconds after she let Carol into her flat. It was two days after Carol's meeting with Sarah.

"How did you know?"

"You look guilty."

"Look, Josie, I think you should agree to meet her."

"I tried before. She blew it. End of story."

"No really, I mentioned the funeral. She truly thought you were Michael's girlfriend. She didn't know who you really were."

"Yep, that'll be right."

"Oh, come on Josie. It was her boy's funeral. You don't know what was going on in her head."

Josie led Carol down the hall, her back to her.

"Mmm, well."

Carol knew this was the beginning of a concession. It would do for now. No point in pushing it.

"How are you keeping Josie? You're getting big."

Josie turned, so that her shape was in silhouette against the light coming from the living room. She pulled her shirt down tight over her belly, emphasising her bump.

"I feel like I'm carrying a portable telly up my

jumper!"

"You certainly look healthier these days. You used to look like death warmed up. And how are all the preparations going?"

"Michael's actually doing up the spare room as we talk. Put your head round the door."

"Oh, I'll just let him get on with it. I'll say cheerio when I'm leaving."

"Suit yourself. It'll only give him an excuse for another cup of tea anyway. Oh, there he is. Talk of the Devil!"

Michael came into the hall, smelling of paint and wet wallpaper. He had on an old boiler suit, too tight for him, which emphasised his broad frame. The sleeves came down as far as his forearms.

"Hello there, Carol. Just going for a pee. Kettle on, Josie?"

"No wonder you've got bladder problems," laughed Josie. "I'm just getting an urn installed in that kitchen, save me wearing out the kettle."

"Wear did you get your boiler suit Michael? The Petite Section of "Workies-R-Us?"

"It's an old one of my Uncle Peter's."

The mention of Josie's father brought about a change of atmosphere. Michael looked sheepish and squeezed past them wordlessly.

Carol followed Josie into the kitchen. She was putting tea bags into the kettle, instead of the teapot.

"Need any help, Josie?"

"No, you're all right. Away through to the living room."

Carol took the hint. She decided to leave Josie to sort herself out for a few minutes.

As she was leafing through a magazine she'd found on the settee, Michael came in.

"Is she still through in the kitchen?"

His voice was a low murmur.

"Yes," replied Carol, in the same hushed tone, "she sounded a bit upset."

"I shouldnae have mentioned her da. Stupid."

"Is he still not speaking to her?"

"No' speaking! Paps me oot the hoose if I even mention Jim's or her name."

"But he gave you a boiler suit?"

"*Sold* me a boiler suit. He thinks I'm working on my motor."

"If he was so set against Robert, surely he'd soften now the poor boy's dead?"

Carol saw a look pass over Michael's face. Just for a second, she'd forgotten that he and Robert had been best pals.

"Rab is just an excuse to keep it going. He fell out with Josie for other reasons. Did you know she lived with Jim before she got this place?"

Carol wanted to ask what Josie could have done to her father, but she felt she would be taking advantage of Michael's inability to be discreet. It was him, after all, who'd let on she was pregnant. This time, she wanted to be told by Josie, or not at all.

Which was just as well, as Josie was standing in the doorway, tray in hand.

"Michael, why don't you just go through my knickers drawer? Then you could put a notice in the foyer about what colour they are."

Michael flushed from his hair to somewhere underneath his collar.

"I'm sorry, Josie."

"You couldnae hold your own water."

"I know, I know, I'm really sorry. Can I just take my tea through to the bedroom?"

Josie held out a mug.

"Here, take it and scram. Don't choke on it, mind!"

Josie handed Carol another mug.

"I'm sorry, Carol. I meant to go into town to get you a nice bottle of wine, but with running about after Michael I never got the time."

"That's OK, Josie. I had enough to drink at the Quiz Night. I'm drying out for a while."

Josie lowered herself into a settee opposite Carol.

"Oh, that's right – how did you get on with Jim?"

"Em – well – he left a bit early."

"That's not like him."

There was a silence for a few minutes, both women staring at the drink in their hand. Josie suddenly slapped her mug down on the table.

"Me dear oul' da – that'll be fucking right! We all lived in a nice house in Kings Park, respectable area, back and front garden. What a bloody façade! He used to belt us all. Jim got it the worst, 'cos he wouldn't keep quiet. Michael was the only one he was nice to."

"I didn't know Michael lived with you."

It was an irrelevant remark, but she couldn't think what else to say.

"We weren't allowed to talk about it, but Michael never had a dad. His mum, my Auntie Bridget, lived with us 'cos she'd nowhere else to go. Believe me, if you stayed with us, you *really* did have nowhere to go. She was knocked down and killed when Michael was ten."

Carol just gave in at this point, and let Josie get on with it.

"It got that bad that Jim dropped out of Uni so he could get a job and leave home. He'd wanted a job in computers, but couldn't get one because he never finished his course. That's when he ended up in the butchers. He was about nineteen, I think. I was fourteen; Michael was a couple of years older than me. Jim tried to get us and my mum to come with him but she wouldn't leave her man. She kept saying that we didn't know him when he was young, when he laughed all the time. She was sure he was going to change back. It's not even as if he bevvied. He was tea-total. Just a bad tempered old bastard."

Carol nodded.

"I think my mum knew she was going to get cancer. They say breast cancer is hereditary, and my granny died from it, shortly after she had my mum. She'd only one other wee one, my Uncle James. I've never met him. He went to Australia about thirty years ago. The point was that my mum knew that when she died, the only real adult left in the family would be my dad."

Josie uncovered her face, looked at Carol, trying to get her to understand something.

"She never went to the doctor until it was too late. As well as a savings account, she'd taken out a policy you see, and she must have known they'd check her records, so she couldn't let on she wasn't well. She was five stone when she died, a year and a half later. Me, Jim and Michael were left four thousand pounds each."

Josie sipped her tea.

"She never left anything to my dad. He went nuts. Demanded me and Michael's share as our 'keep', said mum had used his cash to pay the policy and to put money away in the bank. Michael shared it with him but said he needed the rest to save up to go to University. We couldn't believe he let him away with that one. Maybe he needed Michael to replace Jim as the family student. For the sake of the neighbours"

Josie sat back, and rubbed her belly.

"Anyway, one day during all this kerfuffle, when my dad was at Mass, I put all my clothes on and walked out. You should have seen me. I looked like the Michelin man! I took mum's jewellery as well. I'd already phoned Jim and he was parked round the corner, in his new car. When he saw me coming down the street he drove up and I dived in. I was so terrified that my dad would come back and catch me. I'd promised to give him my money the next day, but I couldn't, could I? Mum had suffered agony for us to get that money, it was my escape fund. No way was he getting it. He'd given Michael's money to Father Cavanagh, for the Church. He did that sort of thing, sooked up to the priests, put on the pious family man face. Anyway. I went to live with Jim here in the Gorbals."

Carol remembered something Michael had said, about Josie being flung out the house by her father.

"Did you go back to see your dad?"

"I had to. I was still at school, and I didn't want him turning up there to give me a showing up. I got Jim to take me back the next day, so I could tell him where I was living. I should've known better. He chased me into the street. All the neighbours keeking out of their windows, enjoying the scandal. He didn't want them to know why his entire family had left him, so he started calling me for everything.

"Where was Michael during this?"

"After my mum died he got a labouring job up north. Anyway, Jim got out of the car when he heard what my dad was saying and dad went for him. Only this time Jim was able for him, he wasn't a wee boy any more. I remember the guy next door coming out and dragging Jim off him, and his stupid wife going on about me and Jim being a damned disgrace to our poor father, him just lost his wife an' all. We just got in the car and left him out in the street. Never seen him since, neither has Jim. Only Michael keeps up with him."

Josie took a deep breath, and struggled to sit up.

"Wow, what a kick that was! So, to cut it short, a while later I went to Uni, moved in here, met Robbie through Michael and here I am."

"Are you going back to Uni?"

"I don't see how I can. Who's going to look after the baby? Jim? Michael? Not very likely is it?"

"What about your money? Would that not pay for a nursery until you qualified and got a job?"

"Used it up to buy stuff for the house and just for day-to-day living. No student grants these days. Just loans. There's about one pound fifty left, and an electricity bill due in.

"So what are you going to do?"

"Go on the Social for a few years until the wean goes to school and then see if the Uni will take me back."

"That seems such a waste of the next five years of your life."

"Not really. I'll be bringing up a child. Rob's child. *Your* wee cousin."

There was a rattle at the letterbox.

"Oh, that's Jim. He keeps bringing up parcels of meat. If I don't have mad cow disease yet it's only a matter of time."

Josie struggled to get off the settee.

"I'll let him in Josie, you stay where you are."

Carol went down the hall to answer the door. As she passed the bedroom, she could hear Michael working away at pasting. He was still keeping a low profile, obviously fearing his cousin's wrath.

The door rattled again.

"Patience, patience, I'm coming."

The rattling stopped suddenly, as did the noisy whistling that had accompanied it. Carol opened the door, in time to catch Jim combing his hair with his fingers.

"Carol. How you doin'?"

"I'm doing OK. How are you? Recovered from the Quiz Night?"

He looked straight at her.

"What do you mean?"

"You were quite puggled when you left. And you kept your jacket on the whole night."

"Oh, that. Aye, I'd a bit of a chill. Better now, tho'"

He was still standing in the doorway.

"You better come in then, in case you get a relapse out here in the cold landing. Josie's expecting you. I've only popped up for a minute to deliver a message."

He walked past her and up the long hall.

"Aye, I cannae hang around either. I'll get you out."

"Michael's in."

"Still doing up the wean's room? Big chancer. I hope she's not paying him by the hour."

"No, she's paying me in your knocked off sausages. When are you gonnae give's a hand here?"

This was from Michael, obviously recovered, by the size of his grin as he stuck his head into the corridor.

"Heh, I'm a working man, an' a taxpayer to boot. Not a layabout student scrounger with plenty time on his hands."

Josie came in to the corridor.

"Josie, sweetheart, I've brought your iron supplements. Fry them up with mushrooms and onions and don't give any to Mick 'til he's done a hand's turn."

"That sounds like an idea, Jim. I could make some just now. Would you like some? You as well Carol?"

"I've got to get back, Josie. I've got stuff to do in the flat."

"Me as well darlin'. Plans."

Josie looked at Carol and then Jim.

"OK. See you both. Me and Michael'll just eat your share. Won't we, you big galloot?"

Michael looked relieved to be forgiven.

"Sure thing, Josie. You're the boss."

Out in the landing, Jim and Carol were silent as they stood waiting for the lift. Jim seemed to find the graffiti especially interesting.

"Are you in a big rush to get back then?" he asked her, whilst still looking at the walls.

"I am a bit. But as well as that, I didn't fancy a big dinner. I'm trying to lose a bit of weight."

He looked her up and down.

"Don't lose too much. There's nothing worse than a skinny woman."

"I'll take that as a compliment, will I?"

He looked like he was about to say something, then changed his mind. He turned to look at the lift door.

"Can I ask you a favour, Carol?"

Carol's stomach did a little flip. She tried to keep her voice steady.

"Depends. What is it?"

"I'll shortly be going away for a few days, and I need somebody to feed my cat. I'd ask Josie but she's too tired."

"That's the favour?"

"Aye."

"*You've* got a cat?"

"Aye."

"What kind of cat?"

"The usual. Furry. Malicious. Pisses on the video when she disnae get her own way."

Ten minutes later, they were at Jim's front door. He had a one bedroom flat in the multi's on Rutherglen Road. As he got his keys out, she heard a scratching and meowing. Jim unlocked his front door and the noise increased.

"Hello, wee Cairo. Aye, don't fret, I hear you.

I've brought your supper. We've a visitor too. Come in, Carol, come in."

Jim walked down his hall, trying to avoid a wee black and white cat which was rubbing in and out of his legs, its cast hairs showing up immediately on his trouser legs.

"Take a seat in the living room, 'til I feed this creature."

Jim disappeared into the kitchen, accompanied by the impatient scolding of a hungry cat. As Carol stood in the hall, trying to guess where the living room was, she heard Jim rapidly chopping something, then the rattle of the cat's bowl, as the meat was thrown in. He appeared in the doorway.

"Sorry, the living room's on the right there, second door down. I'm away to get changed, I'll be through in a minute."

He headed for a room near the front door. The cat, which had followed him out of the kitchen, took one look at Carol and scampered after her owner.

The living room walls were plain white. The only furniture in the room, apart from the telly and hi-fi, was a tatty leather settee, a coffee table and a desk, strewn with papers. She went over, to see what was written on them, but they were face down. She heard a noise and turned to see Jim watching her, from the settee. She hadn't heard him come in: he was barefooted, wearing jeans and a white tee shirt hanging down outside his trousers. His cat was lying on her back in his lap. He touched the cat's belly and she grabbed his hand in her paws, playfully scratching and biting, but he didn't seem to notice, as he looked at Carol. As she met his eyes, she tried to remember what underwear she'd put on that day. She'd put her best stuff on for the Quiz Night, and it now lay in the dirty washing basket, in a damp but frustrated little tangle.

"So. You're going away for a weekend."

"Aye. Away to see a pal."

"Oh."

He was still looking at her. She was suddenly quite nervous, so she blurted out:

"Did you ever meet Robert?"

"A few times. Josie had only been going with him for a few months before he died. To be quite honest, I was expecting it to fizzle out."

"*Really*? That's not the impression I get from Josie."

"She's kidding herself on, but there's no point in contradicting her now, is there?"

"Well, what makes you so sure that you're in the right?"

"Well, for one thing, Mick was always with them, and they didnae seem to mind that. If they were love's young dream they'd have been off on their own more often."

Carol thought of the photograph on the beach. Josephine and Robert, but taken by Michael. He must have gone on the trip with them. It looked like Morar or somewhere, not a place where you went there and back in a day.

"Maybe they knew themselves that there was no great romance and they kept Michael for company. In case they got bored with each other."

"Aye. Maybe."

He suddenly lifted the cat off his lap and put her on a cushion beside him.

"Right, I'd better get you those keys. I keep her food in a plastic box in the fridge. Best of meat – the one good thing about being a butcher. Mind you cut it up or she drags it all over the floor. Don't worry about the litter tray – I bought a self cleaning one, if such a thing exists. Should do for a few days anyway."

When he left the room, the cat plumped up the cushion with her open claws and settled herself down on it. No wonder the settee was ragged. Cairo had an insolent stare, which she turned full blast on Carol. Yet Jim had tickled her belly. She could have wrung her furry little neck.

"Here's the keys then, Carol. I'm not going 'til the twenty-fourth. I'll be back on the twenty-seventh."

By this time they were at the front door.

"What will I do with your keys?"

"Give them to Josie when you're done. There's no hurry, they're spares anyway. Thanks again Carol, you're a pal."

She was through the door and it was closed. He hadn't even walked her to the lift. She looked at his keys. As his last word reverberated round her head, she felt a bit peculiar.

Chapter Nine

Sarah chapped on the door, not sure what kind of welcome she was in for.

Dan hudnae wanted her to go. She could tell by her man's face. Well, to blazes with him.

When the lassie opened the door, Sarah was taken aback by how young she looked. Too young to be left alone in this position, no women round about her.

"Mrs Lawrence. Come on in."

She couldn't think of anything to say in return, so she followed her through the house. When the lassie went away to make the tea, she had a wee look round the living room. She seemed to be a right homebody, the place was immaculate. Nice furniture, too. She could see how her Robbie would have liked that – a woman who'd make a nice home for him, just like his mammy had tried to do.

She'd come for two reasons. Firstly, the wean. She couldnae let it be born and brought up just up the road from her and Dan, and they not be involved with it. The other reason was more complicated. Robbie. She couldn't believe that he was a stranger to her in so many ways. Secret girlfriends. Secret weans. He must have been planning to tell her sometime. She wanted to know what had stopped him.

The lassie came back in with a big tray. Sarah went up to her and stretched her arms out.

"Here hen, give me that. You shouldnae be carrying heavy things in your state."

Sarah took the tray from her and put it on the coffee table. Funny how they were called that – coffee tables. Most folk drank tea, sure.

The lassie slowly lowered herself into a seat. By the look of her, she only had a few weeks left to go.

"You look jiggered hen."

"Thanks."

This wasn't going well. Sarah couldnae think of one sensible thing to say. If she kept this up she'd be in a right guddle. Start again.

"Josie. Josie … do you get called that?"

"My family call me Josie."

"Josie. We've met before. I want to apologise for that. I wisnae at myself."

Apologising straight out seemed to soften her. Sarah could see her swithering.

"No. It's *me* who should be apologising to you. I should have got in touch with you before now."

"Well, we'll start afresh, eh Josie?"

"We'll do that, Mrs Lawrence."

"Just call me Sarah, hen"

"OK."

"Can I ask you a few things, Josie?"

"Sure."

"How long were you going with Robbie?"

"We met at a Christmas party Michael had at his place. But we didn't start going out straight away."

"And Michael's your cousin?"

"Yep. Do you know him well?"

"He's been up to the house with Robbie a few times."

When she was talking about her boy, Sarah would often find herself referring to him as if he was still alive. It was impossible to think of him as someone from her past. He'd always be with her.

"Michael's just finished decorating the baby's room … Ouch!"

From the way the lassie's top was jumping up and down, Sarah thought the wean could be tumbling its wilkies in there.

Would the lassie think her forward if she asked?

"Josie. Can I put my hand on the baby?"

"OK. As long as you come over here."

Sarah stood up and sat down beside the young woman. She reached out a hand and put it on her belly, where the jumping had been going on. She could feel something – was it a wee backside or a heel? Whatever it was, it was moving around, fed up waiting to join the world. Poor wee smout. This wean would be Robbie's future. And Sarah's.

"I can feel your baby, Josie. You'll be glad when it's all by with?"

"It's not due 'til the end of February."

"Is that right? Oh hen, I don't think you'll go that long. Robbie was two weeks early."

"I remember my mum telling me I was a few

days early as well."

"Is your bag packed?"

"Got it ready last week. Just in case."

Sarah wondered who would be with the lassie at the birth. It wisnae an issue in her day, but they made a big thing of that now. Surely no' her brother or cousin? She'd ask another time.

"Do you want me to pour the tea, Josie? It'll be brewed by now."

"Thanks. Just a half cup for me. I'm fed up running to the loo every minute. Have a cake."

"I will. I was cutting back for Christmas, but there's no way I'm losing a stone in that short time, so I might as well indulge myself."

"Fire in, Sarah."

They sat and drank tea and ate cakes in peace and quiet.

"Have you thought of ony names yet?"

"If it's a boy I'll call him Robert."

"Thanks, hen. That would mean a lot to me and my man. It might be a wee lassie though."

"Then she'll be called Kathleen, after my mum."

The first thing that went through Sarah's mind was that Kathleen was a right Catholic name. No mistaking what you are with a name like that. Then she felt rotten for thinking that: if the lassie wanted to call her wean after her mother that was up to her.

"Kathleen's a lovely name, Josie."

Anyway, it might be a boy.

They talked about this, that and the next thing. Where Josie used to live, in King's Park, with a back and front door. How it was a big change living up in a multi - storey. A wee bit about her dad, and her mum. Sarah didn't want to go too deep into Josie's family. Carol had told her it was a bit of a sore point.

They never discussed Robbie's murder.

Before she met the lassie, this was one of the main things she wanted to talk to her about. Did the lassie know if he had any enemies? Was there bad feeling between him and somebody Sarah didn't know? But when she looked at the girl sitting there, she couldn't bring herself to upset the soul. Sarah knew in her heart that the lassie wasn't covering up anything. She'd bide her time, talk to her gradually about the night Robbie died. She was never one for breenging in.

When Sarah stood up to put the tray back in the kitchen, she noticed her watch.

"Oh here, hen. Look at the time. I'd better be getting back, get my man's tea ready."

She picked her coat up off the chair.

"Next time you come Sarah, I promise to hang your coat up. It's all crushed."

"Never mind that hen. It's an old rag anyway. So would you like me to come up another time?"

"I would. You should meet my brother Jim. You already know Michael."

Sarah was pleased she'd made a good imp-ression. She was pleased with the lassie as well.

She had been half-feart that she'd be a wee 'hairy' that Robbie was going with, out of some kind of thrawnness. Sarah would have found it hard to thole her grandwean being dragged up by some wee Gorbals trollop.

After she'd promised to be in touch again the next week, she gave Josie her phone number, 'just in case'. She made her way to the front door. Josie was all smiles. The visit had been a success.

"I want us to keep in touch Josie. I could take you over in a taxi to Brigton. To meet Robert's daddy."

The lassie's face fell.

"Well. We'll see."

Was Brigton really such a bad place? Or was it her man the lassie was trying to avoid? She knew she'd have a hard job getting Dan to visit Josie. Why were folk so bitter? When there was a wee unborn wean caught up in the middle of it all?

When the door shut behind her, Sarah checked out the weather from the landing window. It was a dreich and dreary night, the rain stotting off the folk miles below. She pressed the button for the hoist. She hoped when it arrived there'd be somebody in it. They contraptions aye made her nervous.

Something made Josie wake up. Was it the couple up the stairs? Depending on what time it was, they'd be either trying to shout or shag each other to death. She was bursting for a pee again. She got up. Mother of God! The hallway was freezing, there was a draught coming in under the front door. In the bathroom, she put the light on and checked her watch: nearly half four. Shagging then.

Sitting on the toilet, she dribbled a teaspoonful. For all there was, she should have just peed her jammies instead of getting up in the cold night. It would have been dried by the morning. She felt awful, her gut was burning, just below her throat. Was this heartburn? She hoped she wasn't going to develop this new complaint, just as the morning sickness was finally wearing off.

She flushed the toilet, washed her hands in cold water and scampered back to her room. She had a bottle of antacid liquid in the cabinet beside her bed. The midwife had given her it for her sickness, and it had helped a little. She opened the drawer of the cabinet and rummaged inside. Instead, she found something hard and square. It was her photo album.

Upstairs, the springs were going ten to the dozen, accompanying the rhythmic bashing of the headboard on the wall. It was funny that, the guy, Eddie, couldn't look at her when she met him in the lift, yet here she was, listening in on the most intimate part of his life. Angie was all right though, she was always asking Josie how she was doing, even offered once to get her messages in for her.

Josie wasn't going to get to sleep until they'd finished, so she decided to look through her photos. Sitting up would maybe help her stomach settle as well: she couldn't find the antacid stuff.

She started with the photos of her mum that she'd smuggled out of the house before she left. There was the seventeen year old Kathleen, before she came over from Donegal. She had on a cotton print dress, ankle socks and plimsolls. It must have been windy that day; her hair was flying behind her and whipping over her face. One hand was trying to push the hair away, the other gripping the handlebars of a bike. She was laughing and as Josie studied the photo she could see that Kathleen was balancing the bike on her hips, leaning into it. In a bit of a fankle but happy all the same. Her brother, James, had taken the photo when they were out on a picnic.

There was another one of her with Josie's dad a few years later. They'd met in a hospital: she was a nurse and he was a porter. He'd made her give it up when they got married. The photo must have been taken in a studio. This time Kathleen's hair was short and she was wearing make-up. No cotton dress, this time she was wearing a 'costume': a fitted jacket and skirt, stockings and high-heeled sandals. The pose was very formal, she was sitting, a faint smile on her lips, and her husband was standing, one hand on her shoulder, and staring straight into the camera. It seemed to Josie that his hand was holding her down, in case she jumped up and ran away. Judging by the date on the back of the photo Kathleen would have been about twenty-one. She could have been ten years older.

There were other photos of Josie, Jim and Michael as they were growing up, wearing tight trousers, flares, tight trousers again, depending on the fashion. There was a cracker of Jim, tight denims and a big baggy jumper, in the height of fashion. His hair was longer on the one side, and he was squinting at the camera through a fringe. He'd got the clothes for his Christmas, although Kathleen had been paying for them in a club since the previous April. She'd had to tell *him* that Uncle James had sent the clothes over in a parcel. Her dad was so stupid *and* mean that it never dawned on him that it would be hard to buy woolly jumpers at the height of an Australian summer.

Mammy. Why did she have such a shitty life, when she was such a good person?

She flicked through the album until she came across the photos of her and Rob. Michael had taken most of them, although there were some of Rob alone, that she'd taken. Rob. He was so serious and so good looking. And he was a fresh start for her. But he was also a bit of a mystery man. She'd never been to his house or met his family. Rob had said they'd got heavy with him for going out with a Catholic, especially his dad. She was to meet them when they'd got used to the idea. The old mother seemed used to it now, or was she just after the baby?

Another kick in her belly. The bump couldn't

sleep either. Josie felt sorry for it: brought up in the Gorbals with its mammy on the Social for the foreseeable future. That was never the plan.

Rob and the baby – that had been Josie's plan. Michael had nearly spoilt everything by wanting to 'come clean' about the real state of affairs between Josie and him: about how they were a bit more than cousins. He said he was fed up living a lie, and that the three of them should get together and clear the air. She'd begged him not to, even told him about the baby, against Rob's explicit instructions, but she knew it would only be a question of time before Michael would come out with everything. Then Rob was murdered, and the time for confession was past.

Never once since he'd died, had Josie felt sad. Instead there was only numbness on a good day, depression on others, as if her skin was being stripped away from her, inch by inch, leaving her suffering, exposed and raw.

The thought of it caused another attack of anguish. She rolled up in her bed, legs curled up under her belly. Rob's photo was still in her hand. She let go one long sob that contained all the unhappiness of her life. She couldn't breathe for misery. He'd run for his life to come back to her. He loved her, and they killed him for it.

If only she'd not let him go out that night. He would still be here, in her bed, warm, sleeping, alive. She wished she could bring him back, touch his face, his hair, his body. She reached her hands out, trying to summon his ghost before her.

There was only darkness.

And her daddy.

The flowers had hardly wilted on his wife's grave and he was scratching at her door in the middle of the night. She'd barricaded herself in. But that Saturday when he smashed her face off the headboard, demanding her inheritance money: she knew then she had to get out. It took a while for her to make him understand the money was in the bank and that she'd get it for him first thing Monday morning. When he was at Mass the next day she'd escaped.

So she hadn't lied to Carol, just told her half the story. Not even Jim or Michael knew what her dad was capable of. Especially not Jim. For his own sake. She didn't want him jailed for murder.

She'd only ever wanted to be a normal teenager. To come from a normal home. To become a teacher. To have a husband and children. Why did it have to turn out so twisted? Was there no sense to anything? No good or bad? No punishments, no rewards? Happy life, sad life, no matter, just your luck?

Was that fucking *it*?

She'd left the cabinet drawer open. From where she was lying, it was right in front of her. Josie sat up and put her hand in the drawer. With the other, she slammed the drawer shut as hard as she could. Again and again. Her fingers were throbbing, but the physical pain did nothing to deflect her wretchedness. She roared, trying to empty herself of her misery, but more rushed in to fill its place.

She was without hope.

There was a banging on the front door. A woman shouting through the letterbox.

She heard a louder bang. Two, three times. The sound of splintering wood. By this time Josie was slumped on the floor, her hand jammed in the drawer above her head. Her eyes were sore from crying and her face was burning with the salt from her tears. She was exhausted, limp. Perhaps they were coming to finish her off. She hoped so.

There were people in the hallway. One was definitely a woman. It sounded like the noisy bitch from upstairs. Was Josie ruining their shagging? Too fucking bad.

People in the room. Somebody lifting her hand out of the drawer, carrying her in to the living room. Sweat and spunk. It was him up the stairs – Eddie. A blanket was wrapped around her. She was rocking on the settee, but someone was holding her head. Angie, his wife. In her house-coat, pressing Josie's face in to her bare bosom. She could hear her heartbeat, and smell the heat from her body.

"Shh. Shh, babe. You're gonnae be awright. Don't upset yoursel' like this. You don't want the wean to come before its time."

Her voice was rough and husky, but she was whispering. She turned to her man with a different voice.

"Eddie, stop fuckin' staring. Get across the road to the Jim one. I seen him an' his bampot pal in my work the night, buyin' a load of drink – they'll be steamin' by this time. Drag him up here. *Now*."

* * *

What a day. He'd been up at half five to get a couple of hours in before he started his work. He'd only a few days to go before his weekend jaunt and he'd a lot of stuff to sort out for it. Then he'd been boning and slicing meat all day, which was OK, as it helped him to think. Still, he was cream-crackered now.

He couldnae be arsed making his tea so he was off to the chippie for a pizza supper. Not, however, without stopping by the offie for a few beers.

There was a big queue there, right out the door, and he was standing in the freezing wind, so bad if he was a brass monkey he'd be soldering his balls back on. Then he noticed that wee eejit that had got him stabbed. Mad, mankie white hair, sticking up like he'd been wired into the mains. He'd been seen hanging round the Gorbals ever since, although he didnae live local. And here he was, getting served by Angie. The wee chancer was buying a couple of bottles of Mad Dog (kiwi flavour), another couple of bottles of Buckie and a half dozen Superlagers. Jim wondered how he was going to carry that lot, with him being not even the size of a good shite.

Wee Mags was still insisting that the mankieheided one had owed a few heavy guys some money, hence the applied punishment at Halloween. But he doubted the accuracy of the local jungle drums in this case, as getting rescued from a kicking should have brought on an even sorer one. Something Jim hadnae thought about at the time. Yet the boy was still walking and talking, so maybe they'd got him hawking his arse to pay them back. Altho' you'd need to be one helluva pervert to want a piece of his arse.

Angie was getting him twenty fags when he noticed Jim.

"Ma man! How's it going?"

Mankie-Heid had his arms wide open. Jim had a horrible notion that he was going to walk down the queue to cuddle him. He took a step back, put his hands in the air, palms facing out.

"No, you're all right there, honest."

Mankie-Heid clenched his fist over his heart, like some Comanche in a John Wayne film.

"I owe you. You saved my life man. Whit can I do for you? Only name it, and it shall be done."

By this time the whole queue was watching his antics. A couple of wee lassies were giggling at him. Jim turned round to them.

"What youse in for, lassies?"

"What's it to you mister?"

"Just tell us."

"Two litres of coca cola and a bottle of vodka."

"And a big bag a' Hula Hoops."

He'd seen them around. Short skirts, nae tights,

corned beef legs with hanging about the bottom of the flats in the freezing wind. Bum freezer jackets and their wee diddies hingin' oot their shiny boob tubes.

"They're strict in here. You'll no' get served. See that wee fair-heided guy at the top of the queue? He'll get your bevy for you. Just go an' tell him Jim says."

They looked at him with suspicion. Probably thought he was some dirty old geezer wanting to get them up the back stairs for a knee trembler.

"Just go and tell him. That's all you need to do. Then away to your party."

Jim called out to Mankie:

"Here, these two young ladies are in a rush. Get their drink in for them and that's us squared up."

"Right oh, man."

Mankie ordered their bottles and their Hula Hoops. As they were leaving the shop with their carry out, one of them turned round and blew him a kiss.

"Thanks, mister."

"Nae bother, lassies. Take care of yourselves."

There was some kind of hassle at the counter. Name of fuck, was that moron trying to pay with a credit card? So that was his scam. But what shop assistant would be taken in by that parcel of fuck-ups? Did he think he looked like Donald fuckin' Trump? More like Donald fuckin' Duck.

"And I'm tellin' *you*. See if this is your card, I'm Posh Spice. D'you think I came up the Clyde in a banana boat? I'm keeping this and callin' the cops."

Mankie-Heid looked gutted.

"Lady, lady. Sweet lady. Please don't. Think how embarrassed you'll be when you find out I'm a millionaire."

That knob-end was just annoying her now. At this fucking rate Jim would get his drink in time for Christmas. He pushed up to the front of the queue.

"Angie, hen."

"You! What've you got to do with this?"

"I'll pay. Put in six cans of heavy and I'll pay for the whole cargo."

"Aye, so I will! This guy here tried to con me!"

It wisnae so much the dodgy credit card as the fact he'd tried to pass it on to Angie. The woman wisnae daft. And she had her pride. A wee moment of what might have been flashed before him. He hoped that Eddie cunt appreciated what he'd got there.

Jim put on his handsome face. It was the one he used when he was trying to impress a woman. All big eyes and serious mouth. He got it off the guy in 'The Blues Brothers'. If only he'd been wearing shades, he could have pulled them off when he looked Angie in the eye.

"Angie. Please. For me."

"D'you think my head buttons up the back?"

He didnae know what to do next. That was his best shot. But it turned out she was having a delayed reaction.

"Thirty four pounds eighty pence. And *he's* barred."

Jim got out his wallet and handed over forty quid. A big fucking chunk of his wages away already. He'd only got them an hour ago.

"Thanks Angie. You're a star."

"Aye, right. Do you see me twinklin'? Nae change by the way. I'm donatin' it to the black babies."

There was a great big glass jar on the counter, behind the iron grille. 'Scottish Catholic International Aid Fund'. Angie forced a fiver and a twenty pence coin through the slot in the top. She looked at Jim.

"Any obs?"

"No, that's fine hen."

Jim turned to Mankie-Heid, who had the good sense to be looking ashamed.

"Let's split before you cost me any more. And don't think you're tannin' all that yoursel', by the way. You can carry the bags."

"Where to, man?"

"My gaff. It's not far from here. What's your name anyway, and what you doin' aye hangin' round the Gorbals? You're startin' to get noticed."

Mankie-Heid looked pleased. Probably had never been so talked about in his life.

"My name's John. And I'm working in a private capacity. Surveillance. Can't talk about it but I'm doing a favour for a very good lady."

"So that night outside the chippie - were you gettin' a doin' in a private capacity?"

"That was other business. Unfinished."

"I think for your sake you should keep it that way."

"I'm sayin' nae mair."

Poor wee guy. Delusional. But he had a carry oot.

Later on, by the time Eddie was hammering his door in with the news about Josie, the two of them were well away with the drink. Couldnae bite their nails.

Chapter Ten

Tam had been in the house again. Archie was sitting in his chair as usual, but the carpet was covered in fag ash, and the empty cans had re-appeared. The very first time Annie had found him, he had been filthy dirty, confused and under nourished. That was during the summer; when Annie had insisted Carol come down to see him. Her dad's appearance had shocked her then, but today was much, much worse.

Annie was bending over him, wanting to know why he had all his Orange regalia on at this time of year, it was only the end of November after all, drunken old besom. Carol was putting the cans into a plastic bag. She didn't want to go near him, she needed a few seconds to get her head round the humiliating and calculated cruelty that had been inflicted on her dad, before she had to just deal with it. She carried the bag down the hall to the door, took a deep breath and then turned to face the situation.

"Mum, stop getting on at him and go and get a neighbour to phone an ambulance."

"What for? You know they'll not take him just for being drunk."

"He's not drunk. Mum, just go, eh?"

"Well, he certainly smells of the drink. That and

the other thing."

"Mrs Quinn's in. I saw her curtains move when we came out of the car. She's got a phone."

"Right, lady, I'm going. What'll I tell them?"

"Say he's had another fall. And keep Old Ma Quinn talking, or she'll be back over here with you."

"You take all your charm from him, you know."

When Annie left, Carol knelt in front of her dad. From a distance, as they'd been walking up the hall, she'd wanted to laugh at his comic figure, but now her heart was breaking for him. He had his sash on. And his white gloves. And his bowler hat. His arm was broken again. His sash smelled of urine yet his trousers were dry. And as she gently lifted his hat, she saw the thick stain of blood on the band, already turning brown. The hat had soaked up the blood as it had flowed from the gash in Archie's crown. Carol had spotted a dried-in line of blood down the side of his face as she'd come into the living room. She guessed Annie hadn't clocked it, but she could see nothing these days. For some reason she'd stopped wearing her glasses.

"C'mon daddy, lets get these things off you now. There's an ambulance coming to take you to the hospital. You'll want to look nice, eh."

She didn't know what to do about the cut on his head. It had stopped bleeding for now. The paramedics could deal with it.

She had to get that fucking sash off him. She gently lifted it over his shoulders, talking to him all the while, and then flung it in a corner. Underneath, the stinking pish had seeped into his woollen tank top. She couldn't move his arms, so she went into her bag and got out her tiny silver scissors, the ones she used to cut threads and carry out other odd jobs.

"Daddy, I'm going to cut your jumper down the back. You'll have to stand up to make it easier for me. It's the only way to get it off, without hurting your arm. Don't worry, but. I'll buy you a new one and bring it up to the hospital."

All this time Archie stared straight ahead and said nothing. She remembered his "Johnny Cash" outfit he used to wear when he and Annie went on the batter: shiny black shoes, black slacks and black over shirt with a satin waistcoat, cowboy-style tie.

* * *

Suddenly, he collapsed. She caught him, but although he weighed nothing, the awkwardness of it all flung her back into his chair, with him in her arms. He was slumped across her knees. Minding his fracture, she pulled him close to her. "The Man in Black". Was this the same guy, only fifteen years later? She rocked back and forth with him, cradling him, grieving. She was sitting like that when Annie came back from Mrs Quinn's.

* * *

Joe, one of the Paramedics who came, was used to this kind of call out, so he just walked through the open front door, rattling the letter box as he went in. He heard a noise from the living room. When he went into the room he saw a middle aged woman sitting on the couch, hands covering her face. But it was the lassie that stopped him in his tracks. She was sitting cradling an old man in her lap, whispering to him. Joe couldn't hear the words. He knew he was wasting precious seconds, but he was riveted. Where had he seen this before? Then a shaft of sunlight hit through a gap in the curtains, lighting up the two figures in the chair, so that they glowed. It dawned on him. She was like Our Lady, holding God when he had been brought down from the cross – like the Pieta in the Vatican. Joe had seen the statue on a mid season city break to Rome.

He heard his partner coming up the hall. Nice guy but a Hun. He quickly genuflected, his back to the door. A holy vision, even in this dump. He was going to start going back to Mass. Big time.

Carol was driving her mother home from the hospital. Her father had been admitted for a few days for observation. Then she remembered Cairo.

"Bloody Hell."

"What is it, hen?"

"Josie's brother. I was supposed to feed his cat this weekend. He's away somewhere."

"Is that the drunk? Sarah's told me all about him. Where is *he* off to?"

Sarah had been to visit Josie every day since she was called out in the middle of the night by Josie's neighbours. Annie had been receiving regular reports about the girl's progress, and now knew everything there was to know about all the members of Josie's family. Sarah and Annie had pursed their lips in smug contempt when Sarah had recounted the bit about Josie's dad giving his money to the *Roman Catholic Church*.

"Aye, that lot are like that. Think they can buy their way into Heaven."

But it was poor Jim who had come off worst. It was just so unfortunate that the only time Sarah had met Jim, he'd been drinking. She'd never met him sober, as Carol had.

"I didn't ask him where he was going. And he's not always drunk. He's actually quite a nice man. And he's good to Josie. He looks after her."

"A nice man! I've never met an alcoholic yet that wasn't a selfish pig."

"Well, that might be true, but how do you know he's an alcoholic?"

"Sarah told me all about him. And how, exactly, was he looking after his sister the night she took a bad turn?"

"How was he to know she'd have a breakdown then?"

Annie was silent for a few seconds but Carol knew she was watching her. She felt her neck and face flushing.

"Anyhow, you seem awfy keen to defend him.

Is there anything going on between you two?"

"No, there is not!"

"But you've got the keys to his house? That strikes me as awfy pally."

"Well, there you are then. Shows what you know."

"Less of the cheek, lady. I'm only thinking of your best interests. I know it's maybe a worry to you not to have a man at your age, but don't throw yourself away on a drunk."

Carol was raging. She pulled into the kerb, one street away from her mother's. The old harridan could walk the rest of the way.

"Look mother, if there's anybody in this car who threw themselves away on a drunk it's not me!"

"There you go again. Losing the rag when I'm only trying to give you advice. Onyway, the point is that your father seemed all right when I married him. But I was just too young and daft to see the signs. You're old enough to know better. Do you really want your weans to be brought up the same way as you were? Never knowing when the next argy bargy session is coming?"

Carol was shaking by this time. But she wasn't sure if Annie was making her angry, or scared. Was Jim just a functioning alcoholic? She *had* seen him very drunk. But she'd seen him sober more often, when he came to visit Josie. And he managed to work full-time. Anyway, Carol was just Jim's 'pal'. All this talk of children was certainly jumping the gun a bit.

"Look mum, just drop it eh? You can make your own way from here. I'll pick you up tomorrow afternoon, and I'll take you up to the hospital for a visit."

Back at the Gorbals, Carol parked in her own space and walked over to Jim's flat. That was another thing she loved about the Gorbals. Everywhere she wanted to be was within walking distance. As she got out the lift she could hear the cat meowing. By the time she got the front door opened, the bloody thing was making a terrible racket.

"Shh, pussycat. Come and get your dinner, shh."

In the kitchen, the cat was all over the worktop, trying to get into the rump steak even as Carol was cutting it up. God, it must be starving. She put the whole steak in a bowl and filled another one with water. The milk might be off by now.

As soon as Cairo got her food, Carol ceased to exist. She decided to check the flat for protest pee-pees. She could clear it up before Jim got back.

All the rooms seemed dry enough. She'd left the bedroom until last. The bed was unmade. Typical man. She heard a rushing noise, and next thing she knew she'd tripped over a warm furry thing and had landed on the crumpled sheets. So Cairo had been following her after all. She lay down on the bed.

"Cairo, puss. Come here, wherever you are."

There was the warm furry thing again, near her face. A meaty whiff, as Cairo tickled Carol's nose with her whiskers. Then a deep rumbling noise: the cat was purring, pleased to have company. She took a few turns about, then curled up in a ball, snuggling into the small of Carol's back.

Carol kicked off her shoes and pulled the bed covers over them both. The purring got louder. She felt as if Jim was in the room. How was that? Then she realised that once Cairo's tang had gone she was breathing him in: the pillows carried the smell of his hair.

What would he say if he saw her here now, in his bed, curled up with his cat? He liked her, she knew that, but the last they'd met he had more or less flung her out. And was he just a younger version of her dad? Annie was right. Carol could never wish her childhood to be repeated with her own children, if she ever had any. But her life had no parallels with Annie's, surely. Carol had been to university, she had a career. She would never have to put up with an abusive drunk, she was empowered. And Jim was always good-humoured, even when he'd been drinking. Her dad would've started a fight in an empty house.

The pillow was wet. Much even to her own surprise, she was crying. Not bawling her eyes out; just crying. She was exhausted. What a day.

* * *

It was dark when she woke up. Someone was in the room. Had she locked the front door? She tried to open both eyes but one was stuck shut, gummed up with mascara and tears. When she rubbed it she saw a hand stretching towards her.

"Hello Goldilocks."

She gave out a scream, and felt, rather than heard, the cat escape from the bed and bolt out the door.

"Heh there, I didnae mean to give you a fright. Just a bit surprised to find a woman in my bed, that's all. I'll let you get up. I'll be in the kitchen."

Then he was gone.

It all happened so quickly, that for a split second Carol wondered if she'd dreamt him. Then she saw the holdall in the corner of the room. She jumped out of bed, and straightened her clothes. Her hair was all over the place, she could tell, as was her make up, if there was any left! She must look like some crazed panda. And how could she have fallen asleep in his bed, like some kind of crazed stalker panda!

Well, he was waiting for her, so she had better go in and apologise. She was going to say sorry, grab her bag and run for it.

But when she stumbled into the hall she smelled frying bacon. She followed the smell into the kitchen, to find two mugs of milky coffee set out on the small table, with a big plate piled up with buttered rolls. Jim was lifting rashers of bacon out of the frying pan with his bare hands, and flicking them onto three side plates. He turned to her.

"Take a seat. Dig into these rolls. They were just being delivered to Sue's when I went in. They're still warm from the bakery."

He tore up the bacon on one of the plates and put it beside the cat's drinking bowl. He put the other two beside the coffee mugs and sat down at the table. Carol took her place.

"What time is it?"

"Half seven."

"I thought you weren't coming back 'til to-morrow."

"Did what I had to do all through the night, and came back early. Don't like to leave Josie for too long these days. I'm pure starving; I'm getting fired into these rolls before they cool down."

Carol observed him as he tucked into his break-fast, a look of contentment on his face, and melted butter trickling down his chin.

"Have you any tomato ketchup?"

He wiped the grease from his chin with the back of his hand, still not looking at her.

"Cupboard above the kettle."

She got up and rummaged in the cupboard. She wondered hopefully if he was looking at her backside, which she had been congratulated for in the past. But when she turned round quickly she found him head tilted back, finishing off his coffee.

She sat back down again and made up her ket-chup and bacon rolls. She took a bite and had to admit they were tasty, but she had to struggle to swallow.

Then she burst out greetin' again. Not like before, girlie weeping, but great big face swelling, eye reddening sobs. She covered her face with her hands.

She felt the table jolt and heard Jim's chair hit the floor. She looked through her fingers and saw him kneeling down beside her, and then she was in his arms. Well, this is what she'd wanted. But not like this. She couldn't even move her hands away – her palms were full of runny snot.

"Here, darlin'. I didnae mean to upset you. I'm sorry if I freaked you out there. I was just trying to be cool. Know what I mean? Trying to act as if my bed's aye hoaching with lovely lassies."

He thought she was scared of him! She would have laughed if she could. In fact, she tried to, but it just came out as another strangulated sob. She felt something soft being pressed against her hands. It was a towel.

"No hankies, I'm afraid. Just blow your nose on that. Go and wash your face, then you can get up the road. Don't worry, there willnae be many people about at this hour on a Sunday morning."

"I don't want to go, you stupid man!"

She grabbed the towel and wiped her face. When she was quite sure every bit of snot had been soaked up, she squinted at him through her puffy eyes. He looked amazed.

"You don't want to go?"

"No."

"Have you moved in then? Is that why you were sleeping in the bed?"

"With all my clothes on? Talk sense."

"Well, what the fuck were you playin' at?"

"Don't swear at me!"

"Don't *swear* at you! I give you a bed for the night, I feed you, I let you snotter all over the one and only guest towel, and then you call me stupid! So, if it's no' me upsetting you then what the fuck *is*?"

"You're always dying to get rid of me!"

"No way – you're always dying to leave!"

"I am not! I stayed the bloody night, didn't I?"

"Cos you thought I wouldnae be here! What was all that about anyway – you got the Bailiffs in or something?"

"Your bed – it smelled of you. I just wanted to be comforted, that's all."

"Comforted? What's happened?"

Then she told him. All about her dad, his life of drunken binges, his decline into senile dementia, and no safe place to be found for him; and about Tam, finally getting a terrible revenge for Archie's taunts, and Carol powerless to help. And then there was Sarah, broken-hearted and trying to live her life through Josie and her baby. Trying to get Robert back, somehow. Her wee cousin Robert, he was more like a wee brother to her when they were kids. He must have been in some sort of trouble and he hadn't even come to her for help.

And all that time, he was coming and going yards away from her front door. She never knew, but then she'd never asked.

It all came pouring out.

"Fuck's sake Carol. You're taking a lot on yourself. I'll need tae make a list. Come on into the living room and have a comfy seat.

He practically lifted her through to the other room. He sat her down and knelt down on the floor in front of her.

"Carol, you've got a lot of worries, but you're no' the cause of any of them. Don't beat yourself up like this."

"But I should have done more to help, I just couldn't wait to leave home and leave everything and everyone behind me."

He grasped her knees with his hands. She could feel his warmth through her trousers.

"Look Carol, you're a really nice person."

A really nice person. Her heart sank and she felt sick.

"And that's why you worry about people. Nobody made you get involved with Josie …"

"Well that's not strictly true …"

"And now you've connected her with Sarah, that's brilliant. The old wife hates me but that's OK. She's just what Josie needs right now. Me and Michael are not much cop at all the woman stuff."

Jim looked down at his fingernails.

"And our da, he'll always be bad to her. It's a long story."

Carol put her hands over his.

"It's OK. I know. Josie told me all about it. About your dad putting her out. Your mum sounded a lovely woman."

"She *was* lovely. Too good for that old bastard. It should have been him that died. She'd have been able to have a life then. I suppose Josie told you what he was like to our ma?"

"She didn't need to go into details. Phew, I thought *my* dad was a nightmare, but there's always somebody worse. I think my own dad was just weak, not really a bad person. He just always took the easy way out – fighting and drinking. My mum should have left him years before she did."

"*Our* mother would never hae left her man. That fucking Catholic thing. Married for life, for better or worse. It was the misery he gave her that brought on her cancer, I don't care what anybody says."

"I think you're right Jim. I think being under stress all the time isn't good for you."

"Do you know what really stresses *me* out? Sometimes I think I'm turning into him."

"In what way?"

"I've got a bad temper, just like he's got."

"And do you go around abusing women and children?"

"Of course I fucking don't. I'll never do that. The first time I even consider doing that I'll top myself."

"Then believe me, you're nothing like your old man."

"How do you know, you've never met him?"

"Just the fact that you understand him and hate what he is means that you'll never be like him. He probably thinks he's the greatest guy in the world."

Jim looked up at her. She was struck again with how pale his green eyes were. Same as Josie.

"You seem to know a lot about him. And me."

"How long have we known each other – two or three months now?"

"Longer."

"Well, is that not long enough to get to know someone?"

Jim let out a dry laugh, stood up and stretched his arms in the air.

"Aye. Maybe. Well, I'm knackered. I'm going to bed for a wee while."

Carol stood up.

"Oh, right, well, I'd better go then."

Jim looked sideways at her.

"Do you want to come with me for a cuddle?"

There it was. Decision time. She'd been asked straight out. She could say yes or she could say no. She knew she was blushing; she could feel her neck and face burning again. She'd burst a blood vessel one day.

"Yes. I do."

"Smashing. Let's go then."

She followed him through to the bedroom. The

first thing Jim did was rummage in the bed for the cat. He picked her up and deposited her in the hall, shutting the bedroom door firmly.

Carol stood watching him, not sure what to do. There was always the chance with this guy that he really did just want to cuddle and then go to sleep.

"You're shaking, Carol."

"It's a wee bit cold in here."

"Is it? C'mere then."

Jim gently pulled her towards him and kissed her eyes, her cheeks, her nose but not her lips. He leaned down slightly and nuzzled her neck, her throat. All the while his hands were by his side. Her arms were round him, but not touching him, unsure what to do until he moved his hands. He seemed in no rush.

His lips moved down to her shirt. He reached up and undid the buttons one by one, kissing the exposed flesh as he did so. He gently pulled her shirt off and then pulled off his sweater. As it was over his head she looked at his body: there were signs that he'd been cut around his ribs and chest, faint now, but surely painful at the time. She rubbed her fingertips over them, and then her lips.

He pressed himself gently against her, enfolding her in his arms. She was still trembling slightly, and found his body warmth comforting. He did nothing for a few seconds, just holding her to him. When she was starting to worry that he'd changed his mind, he slid his hands up her back and undid her bra. He reached round and cupped his hands round her breasts, gently holding her nipples between thumb and forefinger, so that they stiffened.

He moved his hands to her waist and walked backwards, so that he was sitting on the bed and she was standing in front of him. He took a breast in one hand again, but this time covered her nipple with his mouth, moving his tongue over it, pressing on it. The gentleness of his movements made her gasp with excitement. She held his head, pushing it down onto her breast, whilst she kissed his hair.

She wanted to push her hips towards him, but he was keeping the pace slow. She felt her loins melt, her insides loosen, moist with anticipation.

He was undoing the buttons of her trousers, pulling them down so that her pants came with them. If he looked at them he would notice the wet patch.

She stepped out of her shoes and trousers, kicked them across the room. She stood before him, naked. Thank God she'd decided not to put her pop socks on under her trousers, as she usually did in winter. It was worth having cold feet earlier on.

Jim lay back on the bed, undid his belt and buttons and hoisted his hips in the air to pull his jeans down over his buttocks. His boxer shorts and socks went with his trousers, so that he too was naked, his penis pointing to his belly button. Carol leaned over him, gently pinning his shoulders to the bed for a second, a signal for him not to move. On her hands and knees, she brushed her lips around his nipples, his scars and between his ribs, downwards, feeling his body hair against her cheeks and tickling her nose. She licked his penis, feeling it pulse and stiffen even more, before she put it in her mouth. She heard his grunt and looked up at him, still with his penis between her teeth. He was looking at the ceiling and smiling, a smile so beatific Michelangelo could have painted it. He gasped suddenly and pulled her hair, lifting her off him.

"Too quick."

He sat up and laid her on her back. Kissing her properly on the lips for the first time. His hands stroked her breasts, her stomach, and her abdomen. She felt the stomach muscles around her solar plexus jump, as if they'd been given an electric shock. He stopped kissing her for a second and licked his fingers. He needn't have bothered. When he put his hand between her legs, she was wet enough. His other hand was holding her nipple: it hardened so much that it was painful.

His legs were tucked underneath him, his hand still at her genitals. The room was dim, but he was in silhouette against the window, so that with his erection he looked like one of the naughty Greek statues she'd seen on holiday in Corfu.

She moved his hands away and sat up facing him. She took his penis and put it against her belly, then pressed in close to him, so that it was lost between their two bodies. He kissed her again on her mouth, her face, her neck, his breathing heavy, his hands grasping her buttocks.

She knew that was expected of good sex: lots of foreplay followed by as much screwing as she needed to have an orgasm. What was actually happening was that she was so excited that she was in danger of coming before he had put his penis inside her. Role reversal

"Jim. I'm ready. Hold on."

She jumped off the bed, and ran into the living room, looking for her bag. If she'd been in her house she could have got the as yet unused cap and spermicide. But then, what was the point in wrestling with her fanny on the bathroom floor, legs akimbo. She'd a man in the next room for that. She rummaged in the bag. Found them. Right down at the bottom. A packet of condoms so old that the cover on the packet had changed design twice since she'd been given them at the Family Planning. Still within the Expiry Date though.

She ran back through to the bedroom. Jim was under the covers, leaning on one elbow, the other arm under the covers. She wasn't sure where his hand was.

"Had to keep warm while you were out the room, sweetheart."

Did he mean the covers, or the missing hand? No matter. She jumped into bed, brandishing an unwrapped condom.

"You'll need to put this on yourself, Jim. I'm

rubbish at it. Always put it on inside out."

He took the condom from her and gingerly unpeeled it over his erection. He laid her on her back and opened her legs. She waited for him to enter her, but instead he rubbed the end of his penis against her clitoris, so that her excitement flared up again, to what it was before she had to find the contraception. She groaned, again surprised at her lack of inhibitions. He moved off her and sat up on the bed, put a pillow against his back and leaned against the headboard.

"Go on top."

She climbed on top of him, straddling his hips. As he finally entered her, she thought she was going to come there and then, and had to make an effort to stay with it. Either that or she was going to be in the unusual situation of having to fake not having an orgasm. She hoped he was going to be quick.

Her world had shrunk to the region of her body from her thighs, through her loins, to her belly. When she came, she flung her head back. Concentrated pleasure pulsed through her body, making her limbs twitch and shudder. She didn't love this man, but she was now very, *very*, obliged to him.

When the waves of pleasure were dying away and she was near to collapse, Jim gave a final thrust and loud grunt, followed by three smaller thrusts, as if trying to wring himself out. He beamed beatifically again. Was it blasphemous to think that at the height of his sexual gratification, Jim looked like an angel? Probably.

Afterwards, he followed her instructions and wrapped the condom in kitchen roll and hid it at the bottom of the bin. No flushing down the toilet – it strangled the fishes. She heard him going for a pee and then washing himself. The noises of the toilet flushing and him banging around the room were comforting to her. He came back in to the bedroom and climbed into bed beside her.

"Hope you don't mind but I timed myself. Forty five minutes. No bad, eh."

She burst out laughing and threw his boxer shorts at him.

* * *

Later that morning, something made her waken. He wasn't there anymore and neither were his trousers. She couldn't see his jumper. So he'd gone out. No waking up in *his* arms then. She'd leave the spare keys in Josie's after all.

Then the bedroom door slowly opened, giving her the fright of her life. Jim came in, carrying a plate of rolls.

"You were that keen to ravish me, Carol, I never got to finish my breakfast. I don't know about you, but sex makes me Hank Marvin."

He put the plate on the bed and peeled off his clothes before climbing in beside her.

Chapter Eleven

Jim was a man on a mission. It was raining, thank fuck. He could keep his hood up. When he looked through the doorway he realised that he had two choices:

Hood down, chin up, blag it out, nobody'd pay any attention to him.

Hood up, head down, look like a dirty old man, have every worker in the shop staring at him.

He put his hood down.

He decided to play it cool. He tried to tell himself it was just like going into the record shop up the road. No big deal. He'd every right to be there.

Except that in the record shop his pulse didnae race like this, and his hearing wisnae affected by the blood rushing to his head. He was having an attack of that syndrome, what was it called? "Fight or flight". Fight's happen, and flight was looking attractive but he wisnae leaving 'til he'd got what he came for. Anyway, what was the worst they could do to him?

Right. He was through the door. He was in.

The first thing he noticed was the number of couples wandering around, hand in hand, checking out the merchandise. He wished he'd been able to ask Carol to come in with him. She could have picked whatever she liked. Anything. He'd have paid for it. Back to his place for a spot of modelling and grateful nookie. But she had told him to pick a Christmas present for her by himself, and that it had to be a surprise. Hopefully this is what she had in mind.

He looked along the displays of underwear. When he'd heard customers in his own shop talking about the parties they went to, to buy this stuff, he thought it would be completely filthy. He'd meant to just pass by this place, but when he'd glanced in the window, he'd noticed that some of the stuff was quite decent looking. Lacy an' all that. Romantic even. He'd thought it would be all split beaver and nipple clamps.

He saw what he was gonnae buy. Right, that was it, he was buying the cream lacy bra with matching thong and sussies. The thong looked like it would irritate your shugh. Must be the style, but. He'd seen Carol wear one. They were still at that stage where she was wearing nice underwear. He hoped it would last a bit longer.

But what size? If he bought it too big she might think he was calling her fat. If it was too wee she might think he was calling her fat. She was a size twelve. He'd checked her blouse when it was over the chair, but these bras had labels saying things like 36A or 38B. This was getting fucking complicated.

"Are you needing any help there?"

The sales lassie had on a Santa hat, the pom-pom's of which were bobbing along with her every word. She was smiling at him as if it was the most natural thing in the world that he was rummaging through a load of naughty knickers.

"No, I'm OK, hen."

She didnae believe him. She just kept smiling at him, her head to one side and the pompom's coorying into her neck.

"Well, actually, could you tell me what a size twelve would be here?"

"You should be all right with a 36B but if it's not suitable you can always exchange it. It'll be no bother. Will I take it to the cash desk for you?"

"No. Thanks but. I'll have a look round and come back for them."

Jesus lumpen fuck! What did he say that for? He knew what he was buying, how could he not have followed her to the till, paid up and fucked off. But that would be drawing attention to himself, to how he couldnae even buy Christmas scanties without a wee lassie to help him. Now he was gonnae have to wander round for a bit, to keep his story straight.

He went up the back of the shop, avoiding the eyes of the folk he passed. Maybe they'd sell perfume or something. There were rows of something anyway, wee boxes, he couldnae make out the sign right, just the word "toys".

Up closer, he realised what kind of toys he was dealing with here. He should've turned away quickly, legged it back to the kinky nicks, but he couldnae tear his eyes away.

Vibrators galore. He'd heard of them but never

seen one up close. Some of the couples he'd seen before were riffling through them. They were reading out the labels to each other, like they were buying their bloody groceries.

"What about the "Rampant Rabbit", Claire? It says here "you'll be a happy bunny.""

"But look at this one here, Derek. It's better value. Penile stimulation included. If we got that we could buy the Banana Dick Lick as well."

'Tis the season to be jolly.

He read the blurb for the Purple Pulse: 'prepare to be carried away by ecstasy'. Ecstasy! Judging by the size of it, you'd be more likely to be carried away by an ambulance. He was checking out the Vibromatic Ring when he heard the sales lassie's voice again.

"That's for external use only, remember."

"Eh, what?"

Not only was he going a big bit deaf, but when he looked at her, for a wee second he couldnae see her. He was mortified. His eyes had gone funny with stress.

"The Vibromatic Ring is a good seller", she said, with the pompoms nodding in agreement, "but it's for penile and clitoral stimulation only. Not for insertion."

And yet she'd a sweet smile, like the statuette of Our Lady that his ma had kept in her alcove.

"Oh, right. Well then. It wisnae for me anyway."

"That's fine. If you give it as a gift, remember to

tell them it's not for internal use."

When she turned away, he went back to the underwear and grabbed the first ones he saw. They looked about the right size. He mimicked his voice in his head: "it wisnae for me anyway!" What a tube! How many times did the lassie hear that in the course of a perv-ridden day?

He joined the queue at the till. He was paying cash. No record of ever being here.

Fuck's sake, they were dead slow at serving. What was the Hampden Roar here? The till was jammed shut with a roll of notes. They were trying to get the drawer open with a screwdriver. They'd have more luck with the Purple Pulse.

Claire and Derek were behind him. He was beginning to feel like they were old mates.

"Have we any batteries in the house sweetheart?"

"Used them all up with the Black Prince."

"Again? This is costing a fortune, we'll need to get rechargeable."

Rechargeable? The dirty middens would be better off with an electric generator.

At last it was his turn to get served. He was handing over his cash when he heard a well known voice. Serenfuckindipity! It was Wee Mags. He casually looked at the doors, as if checking out the weather, and put his hood up. He keeked out from under it. She was in the queue with her sister. He'd never even seen them come in.

"Aye, Margaret. Try they jiggle balls to your

work. They fair get you through the day."

"Whit if they fa' oot?"

"Ach, they'll no' get past your support tights."

He couldnae stand it. He grabbed his receipt from the sales woman and made for the door, stuffing the carrier bag inside his jacket. Outside, he nearly ran over the 'Big Issue' vendor. He gave him a fiver and told him to keep the change.

"Thanks very much sir. God bless ye and have a Cool Yule."

"Aye, same tae yoursel' mate."

He trotted up Sauchiehall Street. He was going in the wrong direction for his bus. So what? He was looking for the nearest decent pub. He needed a few pints to settle his nerves.

Carol better appreciate what he'd just gone through for her.

Chapter Twelve

Grosvenor Hotel, Great Western Road. The firm's night out. As they had been waiting for their taxi to arrive, Patsy and Carol had congratulated each other on how lovely they looked, each decked out in their little black dress. When they were handing their coats in to the Ladies Cloakroom, Carol looked at the women around her, who were dressed to the nines: shiny hair with lots of spangles and glitter; glamorous make up; high-heeled sandals, in defiance of the freezing rain outside; jewellery made up of diamanté, gold or pearls. The small room was overpowered with the scents coming from perfumes, hairsprays and body lotions.

Unfortunately, nearly every other female at the Christmas Party Night had on their own wee black number.

"Mother of God," said Patsy, "What kind of Christmas night out is this? Did Santa peg it? Is this his wake or something?"

She cheered up when she realised they were sharing the main function hall with a division of Strathclyde Police. The place was wall-to-wall with men and women you wouldn't mess with.

There was excitement in the air, the welcome expectation of scandal: this was the work's Christmas Do, when office politics were suspended for the night, to be replaced with drinking, flirting with whoever you'd had your eye on all year, married, single, gay, straight or no that fussy. Formal behaviour could be resumed tomorrow, or the next day if you were sleeping it off or lying low in a darkened room to hide a love bite from your man.

There were twenty or so members of staff in Fraser, Templer and Quinn, and during the meal Carol had the bad luck to be sitting beside Gavin. Patsy had deserted her to sit at the end of their long table, which was end-on to one of the Polis ones. She could see her now, flirting like mad. Patsy was attractive: short blonde hair, good skin, straight white teeth. But it was her vivaciousness that was her most attractive feature: if there was fun to be had, Patsy would be right in there, full of life and overflowing with energy. She'd probably still be living it up when she was eighty, the toast of the afternoon tea dances. People didn't faze her: if she didn't like someone she just laughed and moved on.

Carol often wished she could be like Patsy, like right now with Gavin. He'd been throwing back double gins all evening, and was suffering from that common drunken male delusion of being irresistibly attractive just because he was dribbling and talking shite.

"D'you know Carol, you'd be quite fanciable if you just tried to be more pleasing to others."

"What do you mean Gavin?"

"Well, you are a bit uptight, n'est-ce pas? You should try to emulate some of the other girls in the office – they know how to play the game."

"Sorry Gavin, you've lost me there. What game are we talking about?"

"Well, look at Pippa there. How do you think she got to be an Associate, so soon? Not due to her massive intellect, I'm sure."

Carol looked down the table. Pippa was deep in conversation with one of the married senior partners, old enough to be her father. She was looking deep into his eyes, listening to his every word as if he was Jesus on the Mount. Carol could imagine what kind of mounting would be going on there.

She'd always wondered about Pippa, who was a pretty, well brought up middle class girl, charming and confident. Smart, too, and well connected: her father and brother were solicitors. If she hadn't been in so much of a rush, she could have become an Associate on her own merits, and everybody would have known it. Instead she had taken a short cut to promotion, and in the course of her journey had become the butt of derision from dickheads like Gavin. Pippa could have bought and sold Gavin, before the lunch hour; which these days she was spending in five star hotel rooms with old Templer.

"So Gavin, you think I should play the game as well?"

He leaned towards her, reeking of drink, and so close that she could see the broken veins on his

156

nose, and the wee black hairs coming from his nostrils. He had trouble focusing - "one eye up the chimney, and the other up the lum".

"You might find it to your advantage."

"But Gavin," she said, "There's a world of difference between playing the game and being on it."

She stood up and pushed her chair back.

"Pathetic. Drunken. Prick. I wouldn't shag you if you were the Lord Advocate!"

She never heard what he said as she walked away from him.

People were moving away from their seats now that the meal was over, and the band had started playing. She was a prize idiot. She should just have laughed in Gavin's face and walked away. Now that he really knew what she thought about him, he would start getting nasty: he'd nothing to lose.

She went over to Patsy and sat down. She was holding court, surrounded by good looking men.

"Carol hen, sit down and meet the boys. This is Graham, Stuart and Calum. Good Scottish names, eh? What one of you handsome hunks is getting my pal a drink? A dry white wine and soda, no ice."

Patsy took one look at her friend's face.

"We're off to powder our noses. Don't let anyone take our seats, mind!"

The scene in the Ladies toilet was typical of a big Christmas night out. There were women queuing for the cubicles, others putting on lipstick at the mirror and passing round a can of hairspray, about the size of a small fire extinguisher. A young girl was crying in the corner, mascara running down her cheeks, being comforted by her mates, and wiping her snottery nose with her elbow length satin gloves. An older woman was having a pee, talking to her friend with the cubicle door half open, suburban accent but giving the game away by hovering three inches above the seat: obviously brought up in a close with a shared cludgie.

"What's up Carol?"

She told Patsy all about it. And everyone else. She hadn't meant to, but the loo was so crowded that within minutes every woman in the room was demanding more information. The cludgie hoverer, by now with her knickers pulled back up and her skirt pulled down, was even peeking out the main door, trying to find Carol's table, and Gavin, for the benefit of the assembled females.

"Is it that one pet, the wee fat one with the curly hair, with the bottle of brandy in front of him? Yes? It is him? Oh, oh, he's getting up. He's a bit shaky on his pins. Oh no, he's coming over here. No, it's fine, he's just away to the Gents."

The girl who'd been sobbing chimed in.

"The bastard. But then all men are bastards. The ones you think are nice are just devious bastards," she sniffled.

The second part of the evening was a great improvement on the first. Patsy seemed to have a string of men at her beck and call which, being the friend she was, she seemed quite happy to share with Carol. She didn't bother looking too closely at their left hand, as she knew what she would find in most cases: the tell tale pink impression left by a recently removed wedding ring. Still, she wasn't that bothered, she was only dancing.

Anyway, she had a man. Jim. Oh, that first night she'd spent with him! Now she knew what Marvin Gaye meant by 'sexual healing'.

Towards the end of the evening, she found herself sitting all alone. Everyone else was up dancing or at the bar. With a sigh of relief she took off her shoes and wriggled her toes, and put her feet up on a free chair beside her.

"Heh, I was just going to sit there!"

And there he was.

"Jim! What are you doing here?"

"I was at a loose end. Thought I'd help you and your mate to get home. I've got a pal that runs a taxi during the Festive Season. Goes to Florida every year on the takings. I've been here for a while."

Carol squirmed a little.

"I never noticed you."

"I was at the bar. I saw Patsy, and her harem. Have you been enjoying yourself?"

"Em, yeah. Not bad."

She put her shoes back on, aware that he was watching her. She'd nothing to feel guilty about. Nothing.

The band, which up until that moment had

been playing rock and roll and party music, suddenly struck up the music for a Scottish Reel.

"Ladies and gentlemen," announced the band leader, "let's show us what you're made of! Take the floor for a 'Strip the Willow.' We'll talk you through it if you don't know the steps. Let's see you up, ladies and gents. Come on now, the night is still young!"

Still not looking at Jim, Carol instead watched the dance floor, which was suddenly crowded with half-drunk partygoers, lining up in sets of eight to do the dance. The band leader, true to his word, talked them through the steps, section by section.

Just before the music started, six people joined the dance floor: they needed another couple to make a set. Jim grabbed Carol's hand and hoisted her to her feet.

"Right, let's go. You can dance with me now."

She was going to duck out, as her feet were complaining about being back in the stilettos, but instead she found herself at the head of the line, facing Jim. The music started.

She met him in the middle and linked arms. It all came back to her. Jim birled her round, faster and faster. They built up such a speed that they were ahead of the music. Instead of eight steps, she managed ten, but Jim released her in time with the beat. She flew over to the first guy in the line. A big guy, red-headed, no neck and at least eighteen stones. He'd seen how fast she was going: he flicked her back to Jim. She kept her balance. She was enjoying this. Jim birled round with her, laughing now. He passed her to the next man and the next, until the end of the line. He should then have linked arms with her, but instead he grabbed her by the waist and lifted her, spinning round: she felt her feet leave the floor. He was looking up at her and grinning. She clutched his shoulders and held on tight. She knew she was safe.

Their turn was over. As the other dancers took their turn, the music got faster and faster. Men and women were flying all over the place. Carol's breakneck speed a few minutes before caught up with her. She was dizzy and breathless. Still the music played, and she stamped her feet and clapped her hands until they stung. "Nae Neck" came towards her, and she let out a Caledonian whooping yell – the same sound that had the Romans shake in their sandals two thousand years before. "Nae Neck" linked arms and laughed.

The music stopped. Anyone who was still standing headed for the bar. Including Jim. As Carol recovered her breath, she noticed that Gavin was clinging onto the bar, waving a twenty pound note around.

"Nae Neck" came over to Carol. He held out his hand.

"Good on you doll! I like a wumman with spunk."

She smiled at his cheek and shook the offered hand, only to feel as if her arm was to be wrenched from its socket. Out of the corner of her eye, Carol saw Gavin saying something to Jim, whilst pointing his twenty pound note at Carol.

The band was now playing that slow, end of the night music, the one you're supposed to clinch the deal with. Carol stared in horror as Jim strode across the dance floor, followed at arms length by Gavin, who really had no choice in the matter, as Jim had grabbed a fistful of his jacket. They were heading for the Gents.

"Oh, oh. Trouble," said Nae Neck.

'Well, that must be the understatement of the year', thought Carol, as she too made of in the direction of the Gents.

"Where are you going, doll?"

"That's my boyfriend!"

"What, the wee fat one you were sitting beside earlier? The one that tried to touch up one of my colleagues during the Hokey Cokey?"

"No not him. The other one. I think he said something to him about me. He's going to get himself arrested over that tosser. Wait a minute – did you say Gavin tried to molest some man during the Hokey Cokey?"

"I don't think Sandra would be too keen to get referred to as a man. She would have lifted him there and then, but she couldn't be annoyed with the paperwork back at the station."

"You're all the Police?"

"Oh, aye doll. You wait here, and we'll bring your man back."

Nae Neck went over to some of Patsy's new pals and spoke quietly to them, whilst nodding in the direction of the Gents, before they all sauntered over to the toilets.

Patsy came over.

"What's happening?"

"I think Gavin insulted me to Jim, 'cos he's just dragged him into the toilets. Some of the Polis have gone in to break it up, but they're taking ages."

Suddenly the Gents door burst open and Jim came stumbling out, landing on his knees. The band was playing 'Lady in Red'. Jim jumped to his feet and ran back in. They must have been waiting for him, as ten seconds later he flew back out again, this time with his leather jacket pulled down over his shoulders, pinning his arms to his sides.

Carol ran over to him, and put her arms round his waist.

"Jim, Stop it. Now!"

He roughly shook her off and she tottered two steps backward, before one of her high heels caught on the carpet, and she fell flat on her back.

"Christ, Carol. I'm sorry. I didnae mean that to happen."

He was leaning over her, lifting her to her feet. By this time, a small crowd had gathered. She was mortified, and raging.

She stood up, and rotated her ankle. No harm done, except to her pride.

"Jim, just go. I don't want to speak to you now.

Go!"

He didn't move, but just kept holding onto her arm. Carol pulled away from him, pushing him in the chest.

"Would you beat it? I wish you'd never shown your face here tonight! You've spoiled everything."

Patsy was at her side.

"Jim, son, quit while you're ahead. You're not helping matters here. Away home, and I'll make sure she's OK."

"Aye, all right, Patsy. Phone me tomorrow Carol, will you?"

Carol waved him off without a reply. Jim straightened his jacket and walked away.

Patsy took her by the elbow and guided her to a couple of spare seats.

"Carol, come and sit over here. Take this wee vodka for your nerves. What a couple of stupid bastards. See men! I'm away to find out what's happening. Don't you move from that spot."

Nae Neck and his pals were emerging from the toilet. Two of them had their arms round a limping Gavin, supporting him as he made for the cloakroom. Nae Neck said something to Patsy and then gestured a thumbs up sign to Carol.

Patsy cam back over and sat beside Carol.

"Apparently he'll be pissing blood for a week, but he won't be taking this any further. He thinks Jim was one of the Polis, and he doesn't want to get arrested for assault."

"Assault! But Jim set about him!"

"The only witnesses were even more Polis, so Gavin thinks he's onto a loser. He's a bigger bum than ten arses, but he's not completely daft. Anyway, they're going to get him a free lift home. In a squad car. That should get his neighbours talking."

"He'll have my P45 waiting for me tomorrow."

"He won't. I'll have a word with him in the morning. Or whenever he stotes in. Show him the print out I took of his dodgy Internet history. Do you think he'd welcome a phone call to the Law Society about how he uses the firm's time and computers to download porn from S & M sites? Even old Templer keeps his malarkeys for his spare time, and outside the office at that. And then there's the fact that you've now got a cop friend keeping an eye on him."

"I can't believe Jim acted like that!"

"What? But you know what he's like!"

"What do you mean?"

"What about that time after the Pub Quiz?"

"Pub Quiz? The Halloween one? What happened then?"

"Mother of God, Carol! It was the talk of the steamie! Jim fought off four guys that were setting about that John McFarlane. You cannae sit there and tell me you know nothing about it! He even got stabbed in the chest."

"Stabbed!"

"Well, sort of, turned out his jacket protected him, or something like that."

"Why did you not tell me this before?"

"I thought you knew and just never wanted to talk about it. I thought I was being tactful, seeing as you're so 'anti-violence'." Patsy rolled her eyes as she stressed the last word.

Carol sat back in her chair. She didn't feel strong enough to support her own weight. She closed her eyes.

"Just tell me everything Patsy."

"There's not much else to tell. The talk is that Jim can't get rid of John now. Everywhere he goes, John turns up. And Jim only got into the fight because John was getting the doin' of his life. Can you imagine, four guys setting about that wee guy? That wisnae very fair, was it. Nobody knows for sure what he'd done to them."

Carol rubbed her forehead, trying to make the dull pain go away.

"He's involved in a running feud over a girl he slept with," she told Patsy.

"John! A woman shagged *him*? For *nothing*?"

"Apparently. Much to the disgust of her boyfriend, who put him in hospital for his troubles."

"Wow, John as a Casanova! Oh, Jesus, I'm seeing it in my head! It's giving me the heebie jeebies!"

"It's the thought of Jim that's giving me the heebie-jeebies. How can he be getting into fights all over the place and me not know? He seemed so decent."

Patsy leaned over and firmly lifted Carol's

hands from over her face.

"Look at me Carol. He *is* a decent man. You're the most envied lassie in the Gorbals to have bagged Jim McDaid! Do you know how many woman in that pub of his have tried to get off with him?"

"That's another thing. Pubs, drink. My mother thinks he's an alcoholic."

"Maybe he is. It's hard to tell with Scottish men, they all drink too much. Anyway, do you love him?"

"I don't know. I don't know who he is, to love him."

Patsy stood up and held out her hand to Carol.

"Let's go home. We're getting too maudlin here. I hate when conversations get too deep. Anyway, cheer up; we're on a Christmas Night out. They're a bit like weddings – no good unless there's been a right good fight."

As Carol limped after Patsy, she knew something else was annoying her, but couldn't work out what.

When she was drifting off to sleep that night, she suddenly woke up and stared hard at the ceiling. John. Hanging around Jim all the time. That could just be some form of loyalty – she could imagine him being like that. But why had a Brigton boy been in the Gorbals in the first place?

Chapter Thirteen

Christmas Eve. Sarah was wrapping a wee gift for Josie. Just some talcum powder and soap. She held the soap to her nose. It smelled lovely. 'Tea Rose'. Old fashioned, like her. Josie could put it by for the hospital.

Sarah had nearly died when she got that phone call, last month. Half past four. She couldnae make out what the young fella was saying at first, then she quickly realised it was the brother and he was fu'. Then some young woman came on the line. She was a wee bit rough but she'd got the message across. Josie had taken not well and was asking for her. The lassie was gie upset about something and would talk to nobody but Sarah.

What was she supposed to do? What else could she do – she got dressed and phoned a taxi. While she was waiting for it Dan was having three fits and a bad turn. He didnae like his wife running about in the middle of the night, and especially not for Josie - 'There's something no' right aboot that whole family', he'd said. Then he went yon quiet way again and not a peep. Still, he had waited up for her. Even though she didnae get back 'til nine in the morning.

She'd sat up all night with the lassie. Listening, for the most part. That was, once she'd got rid of the welcoming party. The whole jing bang of them.

The hard ticket and her man were easy - they seemed to be dying to get back to their bed anyway. The brother left eventually, although she doubted if he could find his way home. What a state to get himself into. No wonder the lassie had a breakdown. Well, at least Josie had Michael to look after her, he seemed never away frae the place, a good young man that. No wonder Robbie had looked up to him.

Aye, once they had the place to themselves they had a right good talk. The lassie was rambling to start with. All about her mammy and daddy – a bad auld bugger. Unnatural and bad. She calmed down eventually and wanted to talk about Robbie. Sarah told her everything she could remember about her boy when he was a wean, and a young man. Josie didnae seem to know that much about him. Funny that. But then again they'd only been courting a few months before he died.

One thing was for sure though. Josie couldnae go Dan. It wisnae what she said, but it was the look on her face whenever his name was brought up. Whatever impression Robbie had passed on to her about his faither, it wisnae a good one. She didnae want to fall out with the lassie so she let the matter lie. For now anyway.

Then there was that brother of hers. Sarah only visited during the day, as the buses were terrible at night, so he was always at his work. The first and last time she'd clapped eyes on him he was fu'. Yet Josie had told her that he and Carol were an item.

What was Annie thinking about, letting that happen?

She was nearly finished wrapping the present. The gift ribbon was in a bit of a fankle. Dan was sitting over by the fire listening to the football on the wireless and reading his paper at the same time.

"Dan. I need a wee hand here."

"I'm busy."

"You are not. Get o'er here. It'll only take a wee minute. I just need you to hold this present straight."

A deep sigh and a creak of bones as he got up. You'd think he was Methuselah the way he was carrying on. He sat beside her on the couch and put his big hand over the present. She noticed his wedding ring. She'd need to put it into the jewellers to be cleaned - it had gone that dull way again. He never took it off, no matter what mucky thing he was up to.

"I'm just going to fasten the ribbon on with sellotape."

She pulled out a few inches of tape and put it between her teeth to rip it off. Her lipstick went onto the tape but it was the same colour as the wrapping paper so nobody would notice.

"Are you still in a huff then?"

"No point in discussing it. You'll do your ain thing, as always."

"Dan, the lassie's expecting our son's wean. She's all alone in the world, except for two daft young men. What's the problem?"

"Aye, but is she?"

"Is she whit? Expecting or all alone?"

Sarah put the final bit of tape on the parcel. It was right fancy, a shame it was just gonnae get torn up and put in the bin.

"That's no what I mean and you know it."

She actually didnae know what he meant. She took the present off him and walked over to the window to put it in the press. She'd arranged to take a wee jaunt up to Josie's on Boxing Day. As she was putting the present on a shelf it suddenly sunk in what he was saying. Surely he couldnae be so bad minded? This was just no' like him at all. She slammed the door shut and stared at him across the room.

"Are you trying to suggest that wean's no' Robert's?"

"I'm no' suggesting onything. I'm telling you for a straight fact."

"For goodness sake! How would you know?"

He wouldnae look at her. His face was scarlet. She hoped it was burning with shame.

"I know whit that lot are like."

"You know nothing. You've never even met the lassie. Anyway, you liked Michael well enough when he came about the door."

"Aye, that was before I knew what they were all about."

"Dan, you've completely lost me here. Does it stick in your craw that they're Roman Catholics?

And don't make oot you didnae know that. How many *Michael*'s do you know that carry the banner?"

The only answer was a grunt. He was back in his chair, with the paper stuck up as a barrier between them. He was saying no more on the subject.

She couldnae stay in the room with him a minute longer. She went into the hall to get her coat but had to go back into the living room to get her handbag. When he saw she had her coat on, he put the paper down and was going to start, but she cut him off.

"Don't worry yourself. I'm no' goin' to the Gorbals. No' tonight anyway. I'm away to see Annie. I'll be back in an hour or so. If you want to be useful you can peel the tatties for the morrow's dinner."

She was going to walk to Rutherglen to see Annie. She was that angry, she needed the fresh air and the exercise. She needed time to think onyway. She was gonnae have to be tactful when she brought up the subject of her niece's new boyfriend.

Chapter Fourteen

The first person she saw in her father's ward was her mother. Her face was like fizz.

"Where've you been? The visiting time's nearly over!"

"Sorry mum. I couldn't get a parking place. Everybody wants to visit on Christmas Day."

"He's been asking for you."

Carol turned to her dad. When he'd been admitted to hospital in November with a broken clavicle and concussion, x-rays had shown a lung infection. Further investigation revealed his un-even heartbeat, so he'd finally got out of his house and into care. Temporarily, at least. The doctors had pointed out that the Royal Infirmary was an acute emergency hospital, not a nursing home. When his heart rate steadied and his lung infection cleared up he was out. But for now, Annie had had a few weeks rest from looking after him, and Carol had had a few weeks of concentrated harassment of social workers. She'd managed to move him up the list to an emergency case, but that was all. She had to get him out of that house permanently, or Tam would return again and again.

"Hello dad, Merry Christmas to you. How are you keeping?"

"Aye, no bad hen. It's nice and warm here. And I'm away frae your bloody mother. Did you bring any fags?"

"Heh, you," Annie interjected, "you ungrateful auld bugger. You know you're no' allowed to smoke. You cannae even breathe as it is."

"Ach, geez peace you. It's no' doin' *you* any harm is it?"

"It certainly is. It's me that'll be looking after you when the nurses get fed up with you howkin' your lungs up every morning," she turned to Carol, who by now was unloading a carrier bag of fruit and chocolate biscuits into her dad's bedside cabinet, "In the hospital and he's still got my heart roasted."

"He's got a point ma. Chill out. Nagging him won't make him any better."

Annie looked shocked, and stared at her daughter for a long time, before speaking in her best righteous tone, the one she kept for special occasions.

"I've noticed, Carol, that you've become very uncouth recently. I wonder if it's the company you're keeping."

Carol kept her attention on the bedside cabinet, re-arranging the contents.

"D'you know mum, I think *we* should take the fruit home and leave the biscuits. It's all piling up in here and not getting eaten."

"Aye, we'll maybe do that."

The bell rang for the end of visiting. She was off the hook. This time.

Carol was taking Annie back to her house for

Christmas dinner. As she leaned over to kiss her dad goodbye, he grabbed her hand.

"Sure they'll no' send me back home? You're the clever one, you'll no' let them. Sure you willnae, pet?"

"You might have to go home for a wee bit dad, if you get better. But it won't be for long. We'll find you a better place to stay. Where there'll be people to look after you all the time."

"Guid. But it cannae be a place where they let Papes in. Don't get me wrong. I've got nothin' against them. But I wouldnae want to live with them."

Once they'd said their goodbyes and were safely in her car, en route to the Gorbals, Annie turned to her daughter.

"Sarah came over last night for a wee chat."

"So? Did you talk about dad?"

"Amongst other things."

Then there was silence. The journey from the Royal Infirmary to the Gorbals was usually through really heavy traffic, but today the roads were empty. Within twenty minutes they were making their way up the stairs to Carol's flat, Annie at the back, puffing and pechin, and Carol in front, carrying the bag of unwanted fruit, which she nearly dropped, when she saw who was waiting for her at the front door.

"Jim. What a surprise!"

Meaning: "What the hell are you doing here? My mum's ten seconds behind me. How can I hide you in that time?"

"I've not seen you since your work's party. I wanted to explain what happened. Carol, I've missed you."

By now Annie had caught up with them. She looked at Jim, and if she was surprised to see him on her daughter's doorstep, she wasn't showing it.

"So you're the Jim one."

He looked at Annie. He had flushed cheeks.

"That I am hen. And you'll be the auld maw then?"

For a fleeting second, Carol considered throwing herself down the centre stairwell, just to get away from the two of them.

"I'm glad we all know each other now. Mum, hold this bag until I get my keys out. Jim, before you take your coat off, I've got a bag of rubbish in the kitchen. Could you take it down to the bins?"

"Sure darlin'. As long as I get a Christmas kiss."

He was at it, knowing she didn't want a big fuss in front of her mother. She offered up a reluctant cheek, on which he planted an affectionate smacker. She glanced at Annie, who was looking as if they'd just copulated right in front of her.

Once Jim was out the door, she waited for whatever was coming next. But nothing. Annie just took her coat off and sat down in the living room, staring at a switched off television set as if her life depended on it. Carol knew she would crack long before her mother, so she gave in.

"Well. What do you want me to say? I've been seeing Jim, and as you have reminded me on several occasions, I'm old enough to lead my own life."

Annie just kept looking at the telly.

"And what's this ... geezer ... got to offer you? This ... Jim somebody – what's his surname again?"

"You know fine well what his name is, it's the same as Josie's - McDaid. Irish. Catholic. Is that what's bugging you? Are you tempted to have a crack at the Papes, just like father back there in the hospital?"

Annie looked at her and shook her head.

"If you're going out with him to spite your father then you're only cutting off your own nose."

Carol knew where this was leading.

"Look, mum, it's really none of your business."

"No' my business, is it? So it'll be *no' my business* when it all goes haywire and you come greetin' to me"

"God, mother, you're the last person I'd look to for support!"

As soon as she said it, she regretted it.

Annie spoke quietly now.

"D'you think because you've got a big job that you couldnae have my life?"

"I didn't mean it the way it sounded, mum ..."

"All your degrees and all your money'll no' help you when you're having a terrible time of it. A man like that'll give you nothing but grief."

They heard the front door shut. Jim was back.

"I'll be getting away now Carol. Seeing as you've got visitors."

"Don't leave on my account missus."

Jim took his jacket off and threw it down on the settee. He plumped down beside it, arms spread over the back, legs spread wide and feet on the floor. He had a gift wrapped parcel at his feet.

"Mum. Let me drive you home at least. It's freezing outside. There'll be no buses."

"There'll be plenty of taxis on the main road, heading back to the town. I'll get one no bother"

"Not on Christmas Day, you wont."

"I'll take a chance," by this time she was half-way out the door, "think about what I said."

"I'll phone you tomorrow, OK mum?"

Annie's voice came up the stairs.

"If you can find the time."

Carol watched her mother from the living room window. She was right, there were plenty of taxis. Annie disappeared inside one without a backward glance.

She wasn't going to lose her temper. She loosened the tie backs on the curtains.

"Why did you do that?"

"What?"

She still had her back to him, as she pulled the curtains closed.

"Why were you so horrible to my mum?"

"Why was she so frosty to me?"

She made sure there were no gaps to let in a

draught and then she turned to him. He hadn't moved an inch. She had trouble keeping her voice even.

"'Cos she's never heard anything good about you. The only time Sarah has ever seen you, you were full of drink, and now you've met my mum, you're drunk again."

He leant forwards, elbows resting on his knees.

"I'm not drunk. I'd a couple of pints with Mick, when we were up at Josie's, but that's hardly drinking at all."

"A couple? As in two?"

"Well, maybe a wee bit more than that. Fuck's sake Carol, have you joined the Salvation Army or something?"

She sat down across from him. How could she get through to him?

"You're wasting your life with the drink. And when you go under, I won't be pulled down with you. You very nearly got me the sack last week."

He flung himself back on the settee, and laughed dryly.

"Is that why you've never been in touch? Worried about your precious wee job?"

"Wee job! I'm a solicitor for God's sake!"

He spread his arms wide.

"Unlike me, a humble butcher. Is that how you fancy me, do you like a bit of rough, is that it? Are you just biding your time until something better comes along?"

"Do you know that's just about the most in-

179

sulting thing that's ever been said to me? I don't give a monkey's what you do for a living. You're worse than Gavin!"

He leaned forwards, studying her face, which was inches from his. When he spoke, it was hardly above a whisper.

"Do you know what that arsehole said to me?"

"I don't want to know."

She looked away, but he just kept talking.

"He warned me that I would get nowhere with a 'frigid little bitch' like you. That he tried to get your knickers off, but you were holding out for some Senior Partner guy. Just waiting until this guy was finished with the burd he was currently shagging. Then it would be your turn for promotion. How's that for an insult?"

She couldn't see the room. She was literally seeing red. She kicked away the small table that was between them, and loomed over him.

"Couldn't you work out that he was baiting you to get at me? Or did you believe him? Is that what made you attack him? Did you think that was the truth? 'Cos Jim, see if you did, even for a second, you can walk right out that door, and never come back."

He was looking at her without expression. This calm centre of his made her storm all the wilder. She lashed out blindly, slapping his head and shoulders.

"You and me would be finished for ever. In fact, I'd even move out of the area in case I accidentally bumped into you."

He reached up and grabbed her wrists, pulling her down beside him.

"Is that what you really want? Just to fuck off and never come back? Is that why you never phoned? Found a good reason to get rid of me?"

She struggled to get free, but he wouldn't let go of her wrists.

"I never phoned 'cos I was waiting for you to apologise. And now I've argued with my mum over you, even tho' she was probably right."

He released his grip and stood up, reaching for his jacket.

"Well, if you think I'm such a bad guy, let's just finish here and now."

She pulled her skirt straight.

"If that's what you want."

He was still holding his jacket.

"If that's what you want. Is it?"

"I don't know. You scare me."

He put his jacket on.

"Scare you? Now who's being insulting?"

He was going to walk out the door. If he did, she knew he wouldn't be back.

"I want to believe you, but I'm scared that I'm wrong and that my mum is right. She argued with her own mother once. What makes us different?"

Jacket on, he stood over her. He wasn't leaving. Yet.

"Carol. I know some women get it wrong. Jesus Christ, I watched my own mother suffer enough.

181

But we are different. I'm not like my own da, you told me that, and I'm definitely not like yours. Why can't you believe I'm one of the good guys?"

"I told you. I'm scared."

Jim knelt down in front of her and put his arm around her waist.

"You're not a wee lassie. You can trust your instincts by now."

She laughed.

"Annie's always going on about how I'm old enough to know better."

"And you know I'd never hurt you, Carol, never."

She rested her cheek against his hair. It was still damp and smelled of outdoors.

He picked up the table and put it back in position.

"Come with me," he said, taking her hand as he stood up.

They went through to the bedroom. There was no light on, but the room was gently lit by the streetlamps outside. She'd not had the time to put the heating on, so the room was cold. She pulled her clothes off quickly.

"Let's get under the covers. It's freezing in here."

As she climbed into bed she noticed the goosebumps on her arm. She shivered. Jim pulled off his jacket and shirt, loosened his trousers, pulled them down and kicked them into a corner, his pants, socks and shoes still caught up in his trousers. As he jumped into bed beside her, she noticed again the marks on his chest.

She ran her fingers over them.

"What happened to your chest Jim?"

"An escapade that nearly went wrong. Can we talk about it later?"

"No. Let's talk now."

Gently, he pushed her back onto the pillows.

"Later. I promise."

He kissed her on the mouth, his tongue finding hers, then moved down her neck, her breasts, her tummy. She knew where he was headed. She felt her insides melt, as she moved her legs apart to let him in. Teasingly, he moved back up her body, his legs between hers. She looked up at him, expectantly. His body weight was balanced on his arms, the muscles bulging under his pale skin. She remembered when they had danced. The effortless way he had lifted her off her feet.

One of the good guys. How could she let him go?

He slipped his arms behind her, undoing her bra. She sat up and took it off, letting it slip to the floor as she lay back.

A drinker. A fighter. How could she keep him?

He moved his face down, lips brushing her cheeks.

He looked at her, head tilted.

"Do you trust me?"

A moment's hesitation.

"I suppose so."

Jim leaned over her, kissing her neck, her breasts. Without her thinking about it, she wrapped her legs around his hips, but he didn't move.

"You suppose so?"

"Yes. I do."

She felt a little uneasy.

"Why?"

He ran a finger over her lips. She bit it.

He removed his finger and reached down the side of the bed. He picked up her blouse.

"It's not your size." she joked nervously.

"Shh," he said. "Sit up for a second."

She obeyed. He slipped off the chiffon scarf that was tangled up in her blouse, the scarf she had worn round her neck earlier, to keep off the winter chill. He fastened the scarf round her head, covering her eyes. It wasn't tight, but it wasn't going to come off either. He brushed her lips with his fingers again, then laid her down on her back. There was sound like something being pulled against cloth. When he lifted her hands above her head and grasped both her wrists together in his hand, she knew what the sound had been. He buckled her wrists together with his belt, and tied them to the headboard.

Then … nothing. Her ears strained for the slightest sound, but he had left the room. There was a banging about in the hall, and then he came back. She could hear something being plugged into a socket in the wall. Jesus! Then she felt the room warm up. She heard the sharp cracks of expanding metal. He'd brought in the electric heater.

Jim's hands were cold when he came back to bed. She heard him blow on them.

He kissed her on the mouth, then moved down her body, her neck, and her abdomen. With her hands tied above her head she could do nothing. Then she heard paper ripping, and something, maybe cardboard, being pulled apart.

Something warm trickled onto her breasts. What was the smell? Lavender oil. The scent was filling the room. She heard the oil sloshing into Jim's hands. He stroked the oil over her breasts, her stomach. She could hear his breathing becoming heavier as he stroked her body, as she arced up to him.

Slowly, gently, he opened her legs. Then he put his thumb inside her, his index finger stimulating her in long gentle strokes. His thumb was moving inside her, so slowly it was barely discernible. The groan she let out surprised her. She could see nothing, but feel everything.

"Do you trust me?"

"Yes!" she gasped.

She heard fumbling above her head. He was untying the belt from the bed. Her hands were still buckled. She sat up and lifted her hands to remove her makeshift blindfold, and felt a hard, sharp slap across her knuckles.

"Leave it."

There was a short tug on the belt.

"Stand up."

She stood up.

"Walk forward."

She took one faltering step forward, worried she was going to bang into something, then she realised from his breathing that he was right in front of her. His hands were on her shoulders.

She walked forwards, one, two, three, four steps. He was walking backwards, guiding her.

"Stop."

He'd changed position. He pushed her forward slightly, his hand between her shoulder blades. There was something soft against her face. Her dressing gown. It was hanging on the hook on the door. The strap holding her wrists was tugged again, and her arms were being lifted above her head. She felt his naked body leaning against her and heard his slight grunts, his breath in her ear. He was doing something, what was it? Then she knew – he had attached her wrists to the hook.

"Still trust me?"

"Yes."

He lifted her hair and kissed her neck, her shoulders, his hands on the top of her hips. She heard the oil slosh again, and felt it being spread over her buttocks. He was behind her. She felt a hand cup her breast, pulling on her nipple, the other stroking her inner thigh.

There was a noise outside the room. She heard a key in the lock of the outside door. Shit, Patsy was home. She froze, listening, although Jim was still stroking her. She heard Patsy's voice, coming from the hall.

"Carol, you in?"

There was the familiar squeak of the living room door, then Patsy's footsteps coming up the hall. She knocked on the bedroom door.

"Carol, I've got something to tell you. Can I come in?"

A low whisper.

"Send her away."

Carol's voice was strained as she tried to sound sleepily cheerful.

"Patsy, I'm resting just now. Can I see you later?"

There was a couple of seconds delay, then Carol could almost hear the penny drop.

"Oh. Oh. Sorry. I'm away through to the living room. The telly's great tonight. Talk later."

She heard Patsy's footsteps, followed by the living room door being dramatically shut. Then the television being turned on, the sound loud enough surely to bring the neighbours up.

Jim was gone. She heard her wardrobe door opening, and someone pulling at the boxes on the floor. She felt his voice, rather than heard it.

"Lift your foot up."

She did so and he slipped her shoe on her, the stiletto she'd worn to the Christmas Do. He did the same with the other foot. She was two inches taller now, fully nude except for a pair of high heel shoes.

"You'll do anything I say?"

"Yes."

He pressed her against the door with his body, so that her cheek rested against the dressing gown. Then his hands were between her buttocks, separating them. So this was it. She said she would do anything, but she had never done this before. She tried to relax, to loosen up.

"Open your legs."

She moved her legs apart and felt his hand on her hips, pulling her towards him. She felt his knees press against her, as he crouched slightly, to come down to her height. Such was her relief when she felt his penis slip past her backside, and enter her in the usual way, that she bit the dressing gown to cover her cry.

He thrust against her again and again and she thumped off the door, making it rattle on its hinges. She so hoped the downstairs neighbours were out. At least for a few more minutes. With each thrust she felt sensations build up inside her, so that when she finally came, her legs gave way and her whole weight rested on the hook. She felt as if she'd travelled from her body, and was floating in a soft, light airy place. It could only have been a matter of seconds. A noise brought her back, ended her ecstasy. It was Jim's cry as he withdrew from her, and thrust his penis along the cleft between her buttocks, spilling his seed on the small of her back.

He leaned against her for a few seconds, then moved away. When he came back, he wiped her down with something that felt suspiciously like her nightdress. Her arms were starting to ache, and she'd lost the feeling in her hands. When he loosened the belt, she nearly collapsed again. He caught her in his arms, and helped her over to the bed, where he laid her down, took off her shoes and covered her with the duvet. She pushed the cover down, as she wasn't cold anymore.

She felt him unbuckling the belt, then he was rubbing her hands between his. Then he removed her scarf from her eyes. She blinked for a few seconds, trying to adjust to the light, dim as it was. She saw his face, flushed and beaming, as he climbed into bed.

"Listen!"

"What?"

"She's turned the telly down."

Carol snuggled up to him under the covers.

"She didn't give us that long then. Shows what she thinks of you."

She lay on his chest, listening to his breathing, as he fell asleep. She rolled over, draping her arms over the side of the bed, trying to get rid of the pins and needles that were now attacking her. She was in that position when she too drifted off.

When she woke later, she saw Jim's naked form in the semi-darkness. He was unplugging the heater.

"Shouldnae have done that. Fell asleep with the heater on. It's been on full pelt for two hours. Dangerous. The room's like an oven now."

"It smells lovely but. Was that lavender oil?"

"Aye. Got you it for your Christmas. Nearly done now. I'll buy you more. I got you this as well. Hope you like it."

He reached over to the parcel of ripped paper and held up a cream underwear set, straight from the 'whore in distress' range. The material looked like it would bring out her hives, and would probably go grey in the first wash.

"It's lovely Jim. Thanks very much. I just bought you the boring usual."

She rummaged under her bed and brought out the aftershave gift set, which he looked pleased enough about.

"Well, I suppose the fact that it was wrapped meant you werenae chucking me. Just yet."

"No, but I've kept the receipt, so watch your step, laddie."

She was sitting up in bed. He flopped down on his belly beside her, nibbling her neck. She felt her insides start to go wobbly again.

"Do you love me Carol?"

She was suddenly embarrassed by her nakedness. She pulled the duvet over her breasts, and tucked it under her arms.

"Do you have to ask me that, after that interesting little session?"

Jim rolled over, laughing at the ceiling. His penis was showing signs of interest.

"Ha, I surprise myself at times."

"I thought for a moment …"

"What?"

"Nothing."

"That I was gonnae take you up the arse?"

She covered her face with her hands.

"Well, seen as you put it like that, yes."

"D'you know, the thought did cross my mind? But that's not really my scene. I'll leave that to the shirt lifters."

As he lay on his back, she saw the scars on his chest, and remembered.

"I heard you got cut in a fight," she drew her fingers over the pink lines, "is that what these marks are?"

"Somebody tried to stab me, but I got away. It's a long story. Do you fancy a cuppa tea?"

"No. Tell me."

"Nothing to it. I was passing a wee guy who was getting his head kicked in and I couldnae mind my own business. They tried their luck with me, but I was handier, on that occasion. Or maybe I was just lucky."

She was still stroking his chest.

"Maybe Robert thought he'd be lucky, and look what happened to him."

"Carol, I don't go around starting fights."

"So you think Robert did?"

"Mouthing off to a pub full of Huns wisnae a good idea."

"But he was running away. And somebody caught up with him. The Police managed to find out that much. Anyway, the point I'm trying to make is, no matter what the cause is, any fight is dangerous. Robert only suffered one blow to the head and it killed him."

"Exactly. You didnae see the kicking this wee guy was getting. What was I to do?"

"You could have phoned the Police"

He brushed her hand away.

"And they'd have turned up in time to take him away in a body bag. Carol, you've never met this wee guy. He's pathetic."

"I have met him. I know him. He's a client."

"A client? John McFarlane?"

"Yeah, John. In fact, I've known him since he was a toddler. He comes from Brigton, same as me."

He leaned over on one elbow.

"Is that a fact? And does he owe you any favours?"

Carol remembered the ten pound note in the hospital.

"I've helped him out, maybe more than I should have. I feel sorry for him. But as a point of fact, I owe him. It was him that told me how to find Josie, and that made me find you."

He sat up.

"What's he got to do wi' Josie?"

"Nothing. In fact, he was surprised to learn that she even existed. At that time, none of us knew Robert was going to be a daddy. No, it was John that told me to go to Sue's shop, as she knew everything about everybody. Then the very day I went in, so did Josie and that was it."

He leant back against the headboard.

"That's OK then. I don't want him near Josie. The wee guy's a danger to himself, never mind other folk."

"So why do you hang about with him, then?"

"I don't. I just keep bumping into him. Anyway, I've got a feeling it's you he's interested in."

"What? John?"

"Don't get me wrong. I don't mean he wants to give you one. Well, he might, I mean who wouldnae ..."

"Put your shovel down and get to the point."

"It's just he told me he was in the Gorbals doing detective work. He owed a favour to some woman, some 'lady' that he knew. Sounds like you're the one, darlin'."

Carol cringed down under the covers.

"Shit, shit."

"What? What?"

"He's trying to find Robert's girlfriend, that's the favour he's trying to do me. That's why he's hangin' round the Gorbals. You better tell him his mission is well out of date."

Jim sprang out of bed and started pulling his clothes on.

"Don't worry, I'll tell him all right. And I'll give him a kick up the arse for his troubles. As I said, I don't want him near Josie. Or you, for that matter."

Carol got out of bed and grabbed his shoes.

"Jim. He never meant any harm. He was trying to help, that's all. He'll back off if you tell him, you don't need to start on him. Please."

Jim looked at her standing in front of him, clutching a pair of shoes to her naked breasts.

"Aye OK, you're probably right. I'll never find him the night anyway. But when I see him, I'll tell him the score, and give him one chance to fuck off. Christ on a bike, what a fuckin' private eye he'd make! If brains were dynamite he wouldnae have enough to blow his head off."

Carol handed him his shoes. He took them, but didn't put them on.

"What, you throwing me out?"

"Not if you don't want to. I could stay in here forever. Although eventually I'd have to forage for food."

He threw his shoes to the floor.

"Aye, I'm getting a bit peckish. Tell, you what, seeing as I'm dressed, I'll make us something to eat. Don't want to shock your wee pal if she's still hanging about. You could try on your Christmas present, see if it fits you."

"Great idea, I'm dying to try it on."

Maybe she did love him.

Jim more or less ran to the door.

"Right, I'll not be long then. Maybe just a wee snack."

"Fine, but on one condition."

"What's that then?"

"My turn with the scarf."

Chapter Fifteen

Even though it was still bright outside, there was no natural sunlight in the lounge of 'The Spuig'. Instead the smoky room was lit with mock Victorian gas lights; ranged around the wall were landscapes and hunting scenes, lit up by tacky brass highlighters. She'd never really noticed the décor before.

She blinked, looking around for him. Even for a Saturday afternoon, the place was crowded.

"Carol! Over here."

Jim was standing at the bar, a barely sipped pint in front of him. Beside the glass was a beer mat, torn into at least twenty pieces. His holdall was at his feet, like some faithful hound. He see-med to carry it around everywhere these days, although nobody knew what he kept in it. Another thing about him that irritated her.

"What d'you want to drink?"

"A white wine spritzer."

"OK … What is that anyway?"

"A white wine with soda water."

They moved to an empty booth in the corner, all fake leather and mahogany veneer. As she turned, she thought she saw out of the corner of her eye the woman behind the bar, the dark haired buxom one, shoot her a filthy look.

"So what's the big important thing you want to

talk about this time?"

His slightly withering tone put her off, so she answered him like a coward.

"Oh, the usual, just worried about my dad."

The look of relief on his face made her feel guilty and angry.

"I thought he was getting papped into an old folk's home?"

"He's not getting *papped* anywhere. He's on the list for a supported housing complex for *elderly residents* …"

"Aye, an old folk's home …"

"And he should be offered a place within the next few weeks."

"Heh, the old guy's fairly flew up that list! The cold winter must've done in all the *old folk* further up the line!"

They were bickering again. Why did they want to keep winding each other up? It was starting to feel like second nature to her to disapprove of him, to correct him. That wasn't how she wanted to be.

Jim sipped his pint, not looking at her.

"Anyway, what's up with him now?"

"My dad?"

"Who else?"

"He's due out the hospital any day now. They've just ran out of excuses to keep him in. That means he'll be back in his dump of a house until his name comes up for the complex. Today I caught the Tam one trying to get in. He didn't know I'd changed the locks. I had to give him

196

short shrift."

"I thought your uncle's mob were gonnae have a word with him?"

"Well, whatever help they were giving didn't materialise."

Jim took another sip, shrugged his shoulders.

"So much for the brotherhood of Huns."

"Jim, this is serious. That Tam's a psychopath. I'll never forget seeing my dad sitting there in his Orange regalia …"

"*Regalia*, is it? You're pretty much still a wee Hun yourself, Carol".

Surely this wasn't how Jim wanted to be either? Sarcastic and hurtful?

"Listen to me would you! It's not funny. If my dad goes home he'll die. I just know it. Tam torments him for kicks.

"Well, you should watch yourself when you run into that geezer."

"What did you expect me to do? Make him a wee cup of tea? Fill him up with enough liquid so that he could pish on all of us?"

Jim put his pint down. She was holding her glass, wrist resting on the table. He stroked her fingers with his thumb. This small movement was a comfort to her, but then every time he touched her, all her doubts about him vanished, or at least were put away for another time. She drew her hand away.

"Jim. There's something else I want to talk about …"

"Shh. Not now."

"Yes, now. It's got to be."

"No. I mean it." He was looking over her shoulder. "We've got visitors."

"Who?"

"My biggest fan's just come in."

Carol looked towards the door. John had just shambled in, looking all around him. He caught Jim's eye and waved, but there was a moment's hesitancy when he saw Carol, and he looked back over at Jim. Something passed between them, she couldn't quite say what, but he came over anyway.

"James! My main man! Didnae expect to see you in here! And Miss Reid, how's yourself?"

"Carol's fine. We're having a quiet drink."

"Great. I'll get the next round. What're youse having?"

"Put your money away John. We're sorted here."

"Aw man! Come on!"

"Och, all right then. Get us a pint a' heavy and a white wine wi' soda."

As John manoeuvred his way through the crowd to the bar, Carol turned to Jim.

"I thought you were going to send him back to Brigton?"

"I tried. He wouldnae go. He likes it here now. Anyway, I think he's noised up a few heavy guys in Brigton. The Gorbals is better for his health."

"What about the Quiz Night?"

"You cannae blame your indigenous Gorbalites

for that. In fact, it was the heavy guys I've just mentioned, took a detour from Brigton especially for the wee man's entertainment."

"Was it the same gang who put him in the hospital?"

"The very same."

"Do you know, I've never seen a moment's trouble in the Gorbals? Maybe I walk about with my eyes shut."

"I think the point is that you don't walk about at all. You just stay in your nice big flat, looking out the window, congratulating yourself on still being as one with the working classes."

She turned to him to protest at the unfairness of this comment, but he was observing John when he added:

"No' that I can blame you."

The boy had returned, carrying the drinks on a tray. His hands were shaking as he placed the glasses on the table

"John - you're shooglin' thae drinks every-where! Sit doon before you droon us!"

"Sorry Jim man. It's the drought, man. They Police Crackdown's are a pain n the arse. I've no' had a wee spliff in days."

"You should stick to alcohol, you can get that anywhere. Try to get off the wacky baccy before you get totally paranoid."

He ignored Jim, looking wistfully at Carol.

"Ahh, the ganja. Have you ever tried a wee smoke yoursel', Miss Reid?"

Before she could reply, she felt a heavy body flop down beside her, making her glass spill over in her hand.

"Hey McDaid, ya cunt. Still sellin' dodgy meat pies oot the back door?"

The voice belonged to a red faced individual, half – no, wholly - drunk. She'd seen him before, at the Quiz Night.

"Gonnae watch whit your daein' wi' your drink darlin'. Ruining ma good gear here."

Carol's drink had spilled onto his oily overalls. As if to answer a question, he whispered loudly in Carol's ear.

"Mechanic hen. At the bus depot. Not like your man here."

He was breathing stale alcohol fumes over her. He raised his voice.

"Not like you, Jimbo. Real work. No just fucking skiving and scamming. Your round Jimbo?"

"Not for you, Eddie. An' watch your language in front of the lady here."

"Get you! Sittin' here in the fuckin' lounge. Tellin' me no' tae swear!"

Eddie's attention was suddenly drawn to a youth who was walking past.

"Hey Deeko! Picked up any hoors recently?"

The one called Deeko glanced round, but kept on making his way through the crowd. He seemed to shrink slightly.

Jim's face seemed impassive, but Carol noticed

his nostrils slightly widen.

"Did your man here tell you the wee story aboot Deeko?"

Every time she shuffled away from him he moved towards her, until she was jammed against Jim. John, from the other side of the table, could see what was happening.

"Ed, be wise, man. Go away."

"Shut up, ya fuckin' dopeheid! I'm talkin' tae the wumman here."

"So Deeko's in here one Fair Friday. Bevyin' for hours. This hooker walks in, skirt up her arse, love bite oan her tits ..."

"Eddie. She's no' interested."

"Aye she is, Jimbo! Sure you are darlin'?"

"Well, actually, no ..." Carol vainly protested.

"Anyway, Deeko gets talkin' tae her. Takes her hame. His ma's away tae Blackpool for the weekend. Gies her forty quid for the full works ..."

"Eddie, this is a final warnin'."

"But the daft wee bastard's starvin'. Get's the hoor tae make him eggs an chips before they do the dirty deed. So he gets his dinner, drops his troosers – whit d'you think happened next, darlin'?"

Repelled as she was, she couldn't help being interested.

"Don't know, what did happen?"

"His auntie walks in. His ma had got her tae come roon tae cook for him. The auld dear sends the hooker packin', but there was nae refunds for

Deeko."

"Right Eddie, you've tellt us. Now. Fuck. Off."

"We're aw slaggin' him in here next night. Fuckin' dear plate of chips. Mind you, darlin'." He pulled away from Carol, so that he could survey her better. "I'd spend forty quid oan you any night."

Jim leapt to his feet, sending the glasses flying. The lounge was busy, but when Jim jumped up, the customers moved back into an almost perfect semi-circle round the table. He cupped a hand over each of Eddie's ears and lifted him up.

"You. Prick. Outside."

He dragged him towards the door. There were no obstructions, as the crowd cleared a path, seeming to know as a body where the two men were headed. A barman, on hearing the glasses crash, had reached under the counter and pulled out a baseball bat: he watched the men leave and then put it back.

John was returning from the bar, carrying a cloth, and another round of drinks.

"Judge McDaid - I am the Law!"

Carol was shaken. She couldn't live through these kinds of scenes again. Not after all these years. Would Jim ever change? Did the alcohol make him violent, or was he really just like Archie, using the drink as an excuse?

Yet she'd seen the other side of Jim. As long as she lived, she'd never forget Christmas. Independent woman as she was, part of her wanted to just give in, be cared for, as she was that night. But was this the price? Would she have to spend the rest of her life turning a blind eye to these outbreaks? Drinking, fighting and fucking. Did that sum up Jim's life?

She watched John mop up the spilled alcohol.

"I could have stuck up for myself. I hate all this carry on."

"Miss Reid, the Eddie one was out of order. And now he'll be sorry. What's the problem?"

"He was drunk. An easy target."

John looked at her, bewildered.

"D'you know what I first noticed about ma man Jim?"

"I'm surprised you noticed anything. I heard you were getting a kicking when you met."

John looked at her, in a disappointed kind of way.

"I noticed the knife. He'd been stabbed. A blade meant for me. Check out his chest. There'll be marks. He's never mentioned that night to me. Never. They guys werenae easy targets, believe me."

The door opened. Jim came back in and sat at the table wordlessly. If the other customers noticed him, they weren't showing it.

"Right, I'm away to see if there's any gear to be had in this fine city. See you two later."

John held out his arm to Jim at a strange angle. They joined in a handclasp, wrists crossed, hands gripped.

"I'll give you a bell Jim. About the other thing."

Carol and Jim both watched John leave. There was an uncomfortable silence between them.

"You know Jim, don't you, that little scene was totally unnecessary?"

She winced. She hadn't meant to sound so like her mother.

"He was annoying me. They remarks he made to you were to dig me up, they werenae about you. Eddie thinks I fancy his wife, it's been a long term problem of his."

"And do you fancy his wife?"

"I used to. Years ago. Not now, but. Mind you, she's too good for that tosser. The sooner Eddie falls under one of his buses, the better for her."

Their conversation was definitely taking an unexpected turn. There he sat, cold as ice, telling her about fancying married women. Maybe he was having it off with the barmaid, that would explain the funny looks she kept giving Carol.

There was another long silence then Jim let out a deep sigh.

"Carol. What're we doing here?"

"Trying to have a quiet drink, if I remember right."

"You know that's not what I'm talking about."

Her heart was pounding. This was her chance to have the Big Talk, to lay down her terms for her remaining in this relationship. A total change of attitude on his part. No more drinking, and some kind of anger management course. She could find one for him. She took a deep breath, but he spoke first.

"D'you know what Rab said to Josie once, when he was slagging her for going to Mass every Sunday?"

This question threw her completely. She knew he wasn't waiting for an answer. "She'd been trying to explain Holy Communion to him, but he just wisnae getting it. He wisnae even tryin' – "What is this Holy Communion palaver?" he asked her. "You cannae believe that the wine is turning into *His* blood and the bread to *His* body? What bit of body? That's what I'd like to know – *His* heart, *His* kidneys, *His* lungs? You're just eating Jesus, like the Catholic Church is eating you. Superstitious bloody nonsense to keep poor people ignorant and in their place."

Why bring Robert up just now? And she couldn't believe that her cousin would be so intolerant to his girlfriend's beliefs. Even her Aunt Sarah would think twice about coming away with stuff like that.

"Josie was really upset. He wisnae even tryin' to understand how she felt. But do you know what his problem was? He didnae really like Josie. So therefore he couldnae be arsed trying to see the world from her point of view. Maybe he thought he loved her, but he was just too wrapped up in himself. I used to wish she would send him packing, give him the bum's rush."

She felt the blood draining from her face. She

205

tried to speak but couldn't figure out what she wanted to say first.

"He was a selfish wee bastard at times. His mammy had spoilt him somethin' terrible. She'd brought him up to think the sun shone out his arse. If it wasnae for the fact that Josie was so loved up with him I'd have gave him a dig there and then ..."

She found words at last.

"Robert's dead. Don't talk about him like this."

"That's only my opinion mind you. We've all got a different angle on the boy. Mick and old Sarah think he was the greatest thing since sliced bread. I got the feeling, tho', that his da never took any of his nonsense. As for me, I could just about put up with Rab for about half an hour at a time, before he started to get on my nerves."

"Jim. Why are you telling me this?"

"Because, Carol, you don't really like me either. Oh, aye, you like the shagging and all that. And you suppose I've got my good points, I'm not a total waste of space. But be honest, you think I'm going nowhere. I'm frustrated, violent, and a bit of an alky. That's what you really believe, you can't deny it."

"Well maybe, but ..."

"No buts. 'Cos you might be right. But see if you really loved me, you wouldnae judge me. You would just think I was fuckin' great, no matter what. My ma was like that, she'd never hear a word against my da, and he didnae even deserve it. I *am* a good guy, Carol, but no matter how hard you try, you cannae make yourself believe it. Take that wee scene that's just passed. I get rid of a moron that's doing his best to take you down, and you're about to start sherricking me for it. It's just not good enough, Carol."

His voice had gone all wobbly. He took a long swill of his pint, and just kept going until he'd finished it off. His knuckles were white, the glass ready to burst in his grip.

She was overwhelmed by a feeling of unreality. Was she really in 'The Spuig' on a Saturday afternoon, or in some horrible hallucination? Was *she* about to get the bum's rush?

He was waving his hand in front of her face.

"Have you been listening Carol?"

"Yes. You're telling me I'm not good enough for you."

She would've liked to cry, as some sort of release, but nothing was happening in the tears and snotters department. And yet she'd never known a grown woman cry as much as she did. As if reading her thoughts, Jim rummaged around in his pocket, and fished out a paper hankie, which he handed to her. Was she so predictable?

"It's not that you're not good enough for me, Carol. It's like I said, you don't think I'm great, and I want a woman that thinks I am."

"A Stepford wife?"

"A devoted wife. 'Cos I'll be a devoted husband. 'Quid pro quo', that what you legal eagles would call it."

It was then that she understood what she was losing. He stood up to leave, and she grabbed at his arm.

"Jim, don't go, please, please, don't leave like this."

He gently loosened her grip, put her hands in her lap. He picked up his holdall.

"I'll probably see you at Josie's sometime. But don't go up to hers for a wee while, eh? We should give each other some space."

A long time after he'd left, she was still sitting there. She didn't trust her legs if she tried to stand up. Then the barmaid was standing before her, looking at her. The scowl had gone; in fact there was a twinkle in her eye. She picked up Jim's empty glass, and waved it in front of her.

"Sure, you'll be all finished with this, eh?"

* * *

She was waiting for her daddy outside a betting shop in the Main Street. A strange man came out:

"Whit a lovely wee lassie y'are! Is that new shoes, hen?"

Carol was very proud of her new shoes, all shiny with ankle straps. She smiled up at the stranger.

"Ma mummy got me them from the catalogue."

"Did she hen? Here. Don't tell yer mammy." He held out fifty pence.

Carol had been warned not to take anything from strangers. But he was a nice man. As she reached out, he grasped her wrist and leaned over her.

"Whit aboot a wee kiss hen?"

She smelled drink on his breath. But he wasn't holding her tight, so she pulled her arm away easy, and took a big step back the way.

"No. Go away or I'll tell ma daddy."

The man got a fright then.

"Here, it's OK, I didnae mean it, sweetheart. Take the money anyway. I'll no' touch ye!"

The man put the coin down on the pavement between them. As he straightened up, he came face to face with her daddy.

"Whit's your game pal?"

"Nothin, mate, nothin'. I'm leavin'. I never touched her. Did I hen?"

"No, he didnae, daddy."

"Very wise pal."

Her daddy grabbed the man by his tie then flung him against the window of the betting shop. The window didn't break but it made a loud 'Dong! The man reached up to touch the back of his head, to see if it was bleeding.

"That's fur lookin' at her. And this ..." Her daddy wasn't as tall as the man, so his heidie only reached the man's chin. It still made his mouth bleed though. "This is fur talkin' tae her ..."

Chapter Sixteen

Sarah let out a small squeak.

She wasn't having sympathy pains: it was just that she'd made the mistake of taking Josie's hand and telling her to squeeze if she felt any wee twinges.

Josie tried to remember her pre-natal classes: take long deep breaths – fucking hell, there was another one! Wee twinges! No chance – she felt like she'd just been kicked in the fanny, tummy and back. By a striker wearing steel toe capped boots.

Sarah had tears in her eyes by this time.

"Josie, pet. See if you let me go, I'll go and phone round for your brother again."

"Thanks Sarah."

Where was he? He was always disappearing these days.

Josie was half sitting, half lying on a bed in the delivery room. She'd been there ten hours, after her waters broke in Sue's shop. Sue had bustled her into the back, called the hospital and then a taxi. The fluid just kept flooding out of her, no matter how much Sue mopped up, more just kept coming. It had smelled of bleach. When the taxi driver arrived, and saw the situation, he pulled out a bin bag from his boot, with three old bath towels in them, which he spread over the back seat and the floor.

"I've been here before, hen. It's no' so much the giein' birth in the back of the cab that does ma nut in. It's good publicity – ye aye get yer picture in the papers. But it's the cost of getting the seats valeted. The insurance doesnae cover it."

The contractions had started half way to the maternity hospital. The driver was watching Josie's face in his interior mirror. The rest of the journey had been conducted at Warp Factor 12. The Starship Ford Mondeo.

The midwife came in, just as Sarah was heading for the pay phone.

"How are we getting on?"

"I'm in agony!"

They'd strapped a monitor to her tummy, which was measuring the length and strength of the contractions, and feeding the information into a machine at her side, which had a small screen to study the peaks and troughs.

The midwife peered at the screen through her silver rimmed glasses, and laughed. Although she was grey haired, she was one of those glowing with health, strong armed, child bearing hips kind of women. Looked like she'd probably given birth sideways, while milking a cow.

"Och, you've got a fair bit to go, lass. The contractions are mild to moderate at the moment. Did you have a hot bath?"

"Yes."

"And how did you feel after that?"

"Clean."

Another wave of pain passed through her, lasting for minutes, hours, days. The midwife was studying her watch.

"Twenty seconds that one lasted, still very mild, lass."

There was a highland lilt in her voice. Teuchter. Must be one of those mad Wee Free's, who thought painfulness was next to Godliness.

"Have you been remembering your breathing?"

If Josie was quick enough, she could land one on her before she'd even have noticed.

Sarah came back in followed by a doctor.

The doctor was tall and slim, kind of Malaysian looking.

"How are we," she asked, bright and breezily, all dark skin and white teeth.

"*We*, are probably not too bad. *I*, on the other hand, am fucked. When will this be over?"

"Josie, pet, there's no need for this effing and blinding …" protested Sarah, (half heartedly but, even she knew better), "they're only trying to help you."

The midwife never even looked up from the chart she was reading.

"I was explaining to this mum, doctor, that her contractions are still very moderate …"

Sarah breenged in then.

"The lassie's been in labour since early morning, doctor, and nothing's happening. Can you no' give her something to bring her on?"

"Let me check the dilation. Excuse me, James-ina."

The midwife shot her a disapproving look, and stepped back. The doctor gently separated Josie's knees and eased her fingers inside her. Her hand, like the rest of her, was long and thin, thank God. When the contraction came, she barely felt her probing. Not like the turnip fisted midwife, who'd managed to make her nearly jump up to the ceiling with the pain.

The doctor now returned the midwife's disapproving look, with one that said 'we'll discuss this later'.

"The baby's in the breach position. That's why you are in so much discomfort, even with moderate contractions."

All sorts of terrors ran through Josie then.

"Breach? You mean the baby's upside down? What about the cord, could it be round its neck?"

"That's not likely Josephine. However, you may want to consider a caesarean section, as a precaution."

"What happens then?"

"We give you a spinal epidural …"

"That's the thing that takes away all the feeling from the waist down?"

"Yes, although we also …"

"Let's do it. Do I have to sign anything?"

She was sure she heard Jamesina tut.

Chapter Seventeen

That dry ride had cheeked him up for the last time. How was he to know Archie was back in the hospital? He'd been trying to get in, to see where he'd been hoarding his pension money. How was he to know that mental bitch was in the kitchen? She'd opened the door and flew at him, threatening the Polis and all sorts. That was two days ago, but she'd got the better of him for the last time. The next time he saw her, he was gonnae kick her cunt in. Didnae bother him if he got the jail. He'd been inside before. Nae big deal.

Aye. And he'd make sure that auld bastard Archie Reid was watching every move. He'd tie him to his chair, if he had to.

The thought of what he was gonnae do to Archie's daughter was giving Tam a hard on. He zipped up his jacket to cover it.

They'd gied Mary a hoose in Dalmarnock Road. He was heading there for the night. He didnae gie a fuck about restraining orders. He'd boot in the door if she didnae let him in. They could add it to his charge sheet. Anyway, he'd a couple of cans for her. Valentine's present.

He wisnae supposed to know where Mary lived. Fuck sake, his ain wife! Stupid cow didnae change the weans school but, so he just followed them home one day. They'd never have tellt him the address. Brainwashed by their mother.

They lived on the ground floor. The garden was a damned disgrace. Mary was aye a lazy slag. That's how she provoked him so much. Never knew how to keep a house and home.

He jumped into the garden and peered through the window. The weans were still up at this time of night. Whit kind of fuckin mother was she at all? Wan of them must've clocked him 'cos they started pointing at the window and screaming. As soon as he got in there he'd gie them somethin' to greet about. Whit an attitude to adopt with their ain father!

He went into the close and hammered on the door. Mary opened the letterbox, greetin' along with the weans.

"Tam. Go away. I've phoned the Polis."

"Away tae fuck! You cannae afford a phone! C'mon, open the door! I've got a wee surprise for you."

"Your surprise days are over with me Tam. You know you're no allowed near us. They'll lift you!"

"Only if you tell them, ya daft bint!"

Nearly gave the game away there. He'd soft soap her a wee bit. She was that fucking thick she'd fall for it.

"Mary, darlin'. Let me in. It's Valentine's Day. I've got a present."

There was no sound from behind the door. Had they just went back into the room? Ignoring him? Ignorant bastards! He was gonnae kick that door in and then teach them all a fuckin' lesson in manners.

He stood back from the door, so he could take a run at it. Just then, something caught his eye at the end of the close. Was that Raymond? He went to look, just in time to see a back window shut, and the wee bastard leg it up the back green and away through another close. Sleekit cunt. She'd turned they weans against him. He was gonnae bury that can of lager in her heid.

The letterbox opened again.

"Tam, Raymond's away for the Polis. Gonnae please go away!"

She let out one yelp when he leaned down and looked straight fuckin' at her.

"You're for it, darlin'."

Tam knew from past experience that the Polis were slow to come out for domestics. Right enough, the court order might gee them up. He didnae have much time. A window would be quicker. The one round the back would cause less attention. Couldnae move for busybodies these days.

He went back through the close. All that time, he'd never noticed the dark blue van that was parked outside …

Neither had Mary. She was gonnae protect her weans this time. She'd been weak for too long. Every time she got away he found her. This time she was ready. The Polis could take their time.

She'd heard his footsteps move towards the

back of the close. So he was going through a window. Mary wheeled the baby in her pram into the hall cupboard, and told Martin to look after his wee sister. If she woke up in the dark she might be scared, so he was to be brave and sing a wee song to her. Because he was a good boy, he could play with the torch until mammy came back for him. See if he could make a shadow of a dog again.

She crawled into the kitchen, found what she needed and went through to the weans' room. Slowly, she opened the window, then stood up and hid herself behind the curtains. Whatever bit of him came through first, she was gonnae stab. To death. She'd get away with it'. Self defence. They only needed to check with the Social Worker, for fuck's sake.

She waited for ages.

All the heat in the room had gone out the open window. She was frozen stiff. The curtains were blowing in her face, blocking her view.

When she saw his head come through the window, she lunged.

She didnae realise how entangled she was in the curtain. She missed him by six inches. Oh Mary, Mother of God! If he caught her she was dead.

A hand shot out, grabbed her wrist and squeezed, making her drop the knife. She lashed out blindly, couldnae see for her tears.

A failure again. She'd let her weans down again.

She was grabbed from behind. But the usual punch in the throat didnae follow. And then there was a woman's voice.

"Calm down, Mrs Boyle. It's the Police!"

"Mammy! It's Raymond. I flagged down a squad car. You're safe. My da's away!"

Safe! He was still alive. And out there. They'd never be safe.

Chapter Eighteen

When they wheeled her into the operating theatre she took one look at the big lights and wanted to go home. Cancel the birth, she'd changed her mind. But her body thought otherwise. It wanted the baby out, one way or another. There was no going back.

Sarah followed her in. Paper shoes, white gown, plastic hat like a shower cap. Her eyes looked worried over the white mask. She kept her distance at the corner of the room whilst they inserted the syringe into Josie's spine. Blood gushed from the back of her hand when the anaesthetist made a balls-up of putting the drip in. His colleague, a youngish woman, slagged him for his clumsiness. But Josie cared not. Suddenly, her legs had gone all soft and watery, like she'd been dipped in a lovely warm bubble bath. The labour pains evaporated as the epidural took hold.

They laid her down. The female anaesthetist leaned over her with a sewing needle. Like Sarah, she was masked. But she had on a blue tunic and trousers, with a hat to match. Funny what you notice in times of stress.

"Now, Josie. I'm going to give you a few wee pricks, to test the effectiveness of the epidural. Tell me if you feel anything."

What if the epidural wasn't working yet? They

would cut into her belly, with no painkiller! She'd die in agony! She had to play for time.

She watched the anaesthetist jab her gently in the thigh. Nothing. Numbness.

"Could you feel that, Josie?"

"Oh yes."

The woman frowned, little lines appearing in her forehead.

"Strange."

She jabbed Josie again. Better come clean this time, or they might cancel the whole operation. Make the baby come out the old fashioned way.

"No, didn't feel a thing that time."

"Great. Now what about here?"

She'd jabbed her in the side. Nothing. But what if?

"Ouch."

By this time Sarah was sitting beside her as she lay on her back on the table. She took Josie's hand.

"Poor lassie. You're fair trauchled. Listen nurse; is all this carry on really necessary?"

She received a frosty look.

"It's *Doctor* actually."

Oh no! A fight. Right in the middle of her operation. Would she never get this wean out?

"Doctor, look at this," Josie pinched her own skin, just under her boobs, "it's working. I feel no pain."

They put up a wee green curtain over her belly, so she couldn't she what was happening. They were going in.

Women used to die in childbirth all over the shop in the old days. They still did sometimes. What if she was one of them? It could happen. There were no guarantees in this life. Rob had shown her that. And then there was Sarah, poor old dear. She didn't know the half of it.

Josie turned her head, so that she could see Sarah out of the corner of her eye.

"Sarah. I've got something to tell you. It's about me and Michael ..."

But Sarah wasn't listening. Her eyes were on the surgeons. She was more interested in what was happening to Josie's belly, than confession time.

"Sarah. This is important. It's important you know this. If anything happens to me, you must know about Michael. For the baby's sake."

That got her attention. She whipped her head back round. Looked straight into Josie's eyes. She was about three inches away.

"What's Michael to do with my grandchild?"

She was suddenly aware of a familiar sound. She'd heard it before. A kind of low repetitive rhythm. A cross between sawing and ripping. It sounded like Jim was boning a carcass. Then she felt hands inside her. Weird, really weird. The surgeon was leaning on her ribs with one hand, pushing something down towards her belly, and rummaging about inside her with the other. He was trying to push the baby out. The breach baby.

He went out of her line of vision for a second, then reappeared brandishing a wee grey, skinned rabbit. With the biggest penis she'd ever seen.

"We're just going to cut the umbilical cord now Josie. You have a lovely baby girl."

They wrapped the newborn in a blanket and laid her on her chest. Josie looked at the baby's face, which was a wee wrinkled version of its father's.

"Oh my! Oh my! Oh my!" Sarah was struggling to escape her mantra, tears pouring down her face.

"Oh my boy," finally was all she could say.

Chapter Nineteen

Where was he? His heid was throbbing. Some dirty bastard had come at him from behind. He was in pitch darkness. He couldnae breath right. He had something over his heid. And he couldnae get up. What *was* this?

Fuckin' bastards. He tried to move his legs and arms. He was fuckin' tied up! He felt his wrists with his thumb. Some kind of fuckin' plastic strip. Then he realised he was bouncing all o'er the place. He must be in a van or a lorry or something. He tried to sit up, stop his heid bouncing off the floor. Nearly made it, then some cunt kicked him back down again.

"Heh, pal. Whit's going on here?"

Nothing. Then something hard was poked into his balls. He heard a click.

The bouncing stopped. He heard the sound of doors opening and shutting.

Then silence.

Then splashing. Whit was the smell? Petrol!

"I'm telling you. Please. You've got the wrong guy!"

"Commander?"

"Yes?"

Irish.

"Can I recap my instructions, Commander? Are the teeth to be removed after the body has been burnt or before?"

FUCK, FUCK, FUCK! This wisnae happening to him! He couldnae breathe. He pulled and twisted. Plastic biting into his wrists.

"How long have you been a volunteer, O'Donnell?"

"Six months. Sir?"

"Well. Let this be the last time I have to repeat instructions in front of the target."

"Sorry Commander."

"Do you not think it's easier to remove the teeth when they're not squirming around, greetin' for their mammy?"

"Aye sir."

Belfast accent. Provos? But what would they want with him?

"Listen boys, I'm a Catholic, up the RA, eh?"

He was already terrified, but the next words made his blood run cold.

"Thomas Boyle?"

They knew his name.

"No' me pal."

"Don't disgrace yourself man. We know who you are!"

"That's enough, O'Donnell."

"Look. Let me away. I don't know what this is, but I'll no tell. I swear on ma weans' grave. I've heard nothing."

"It really is of no consequence what you've heard, Mr Boyle. You're going nowhere."

"Please. I don't know what this is all about!"

"Thomas Boyle. You were warned off, on several occasions, from the house of Archibald Reid, a brother in the Orange Order. Each time, you ignored these instructions. You are now going to face execution. We look after our own, so we do, Mr Boyle."

That auld cunt Reid never fuckin' mentioned this! But something wisnae right here ...

"You're no' the Orange Order!"

"Strictly speaking, correct. But Mr Reid was highly connected in his younger days."

They were some fuckin' Loyalist mad mob, too mental even for the Lodge!

"Look! I'm really sorry. I never knew. Please let me away. I'll disappear."

A long sigh.

"You've caused a great deal of distress to Brother Reid's family and a great inconvenience to us. Do you think we'd expose ourselves like this, and let *you* walk away? Think straight man!"

"Your Day of Reckoning is upon you, Boyle."

All quiet for a few minutes. They were moving around, getting ready.

"Where will I shoot him Commander?"

"O'Donnell. When we return to the Shankhill you will be sent for further training. If it wasn't for all the good men in prison, you'd still be collecting donations from building sites."

"Yes Commander."

"Shoot him in the legs, arms and the head. Burn the body. Then remove the teeth. Although I doubt this specimen's been near a dentist for years."

This was it. And who'd care? Fuckin. Naebody. He smelled his own mess as he shat himself. He was reduced to the level of auld Reid.

He could feel the heat from the flames. They'd set the place alight already.

"What's keeping you O'Donnell?"

"The rifle's jammed, Commander."

"When did you clean it last?"

"Before we came over, sir."

"Bloody eejit!"

Then his balls exploded in pain. The rifle butt.

"O'Donnell. It'll take too long to beat him to death. We'll be stinkin' of smoke on the ferry back over. Let the flames do their work. He'll have to get used to them anyway, where he's bound for. Get out of here!"

He could hear doors opening again. It got hotter right away. The outside air had fanned the fire. But he didnae hear the doors shutting again. The smoke was in his lungs, burning. Christ, his legs were on fire! He could hear the crackling' of the flames moving up his trousers. How long would he take to die? He wished they'd shot him.

The pain in his legs was intense. He writhed in agony. But his ankles separated! The fire had melted the plastic strips that were holding them!

He stumbled to his feet. Didnae know whit direction to go in. The floor disappeared from under him. He was smashed in the heid and ribs. So they'd come back. They were gonnae kill him after all.

But it was wet. He'd fallen out of the doors! He was outside!

He rolled aboot in the wet ground until he was sure he wisnae on fire any more. His wrists were still tied together, but he brought them up to his head and pulled off the hood. It stank of dried blood.

He was sitting in a puddle, trees all around him, although he could see through them to a field of cows. The place was reekin' with the burning van. It was gonnae blow up, an' take him with it. He got to his feet and staggered through the fields, then collapsed under a hedge. He had to get out of there, before they came back. He couldnae walk properly with his wrists tied, but.

They'd emptied out his pockets. He felt in the lining of his jacket. There it was. Gradually, he worked the pen knife back through the hole and into his pocket. Only a wee one, he'd taken it off auld Reid when he was having a rummage in his house. Do the trick but.

He scraped and scraped at the plastic round his wrists until they were free. He stood up, examined himself. They'd tied his ankles round his cowboy boots. The plastic strips had melted right into them, but hadnae broken through to his skin. His trousers were a stinking mess, charred and smelling of shit. His legs were torture, up in big blisters. But he was alive.

He came out from under the hedge. Through

the darkness and the rain, he could see car lights on a busy road at the other end of the field. He staggered towards them, falling over every few seconds. By the time he got to the road, he was caked in mud.

There was a sign "Stranraer: 5m".

Stranraer! They talked aboot a ferry. He could feel his bowels loosening again. They were still around somewhere near here. They could be watching him right now. Letting him think he'd escaped. He'd better fuckin' shift it.

He ran as fast as he could in the opposite direction of the sign. He got about 50 yards and then puked his guts up in a ditch. Fuck. He was a marked man. He couldnae go back to Glasgow. They'd hunt him down again. Then really do for him. They cunts never made mistakes twice.

London. He could get lost there, the size of the place. And change his name. You didnae need to be official to go skipperin'. All he had to do was hitch a lorry heading for England.

Tam took his jacket off. Tied it round his waist to cover his trousers. He'd dump them as soon as he could find a washing line somewhere. They English deserved to be robbed. Cunts.

Chapter Twenty

"Let this be the last time I have to repeat instructions in front of the target."

"Aye, I know, right, OK!"

"Top laugh, James, my man."

"Just watch what you're doing in that back seat. I don't want you setting fire tae my motor with a hot rock."

"Jim, man, I'm cool. You're cool. What's the problem?"

John was stretched out in the back of the car, skinning up. Jim had insisted on total sobriety for the trip down. John had to drive the van to Stranraer, following Jim's car. They'd bought the van at the auctions for two hundred quid. They couldnae afford to get stopped by the Feds, with no insurance and an out of date tax disc. And a replica shotgun under the passenger seat. Not to mention the fucker in the back. Tied up and hooded, they couldnae exactly claim he was a stow away.

"But Jim, ma man, you should get an Oscar. Pure Robert defucking Nero! Even *I* was pure shiting myself. I was starting to worry that I hadnae brought any pliers! Thought you were gonnae kneecap me, by the way!"

"I have to be honest, there John, copied a lot of it off the telly."

"But man, you were excellent. Pure tribal. Where did you get the name O'Donnell?"

"Just sounded like an Ulster prod name."

"'Commander'. I'm gonnae call you that all the time, noo," laughed John, taking a long draw of his joint.

Jim pulled into the side, braked, turned the engine off, and turned round in his seat.

"John. Once I drop you off, our wee adventure is history. OK? Forgotten history. If I ever even get a hint fae anybody, I'll know who to blame. You."

John put his hands up, palms facing Jim.

"Heh! Keys up, big man. You can rely on me. Ma word is ma bond!"

"It better be. That was serious stuff back there."

"I hear whit you're saying to me man. Loud an' clear. I'll tell you whit but, Jimbo. You're a bit of an old romantic."

That hash must be powerful stuff.

"How?"

"Jim, ma man? You know whit day it is today?"

"Monday"

"Aye, that an' all. But it's Valentine's Day. "

Christ on a bike, he'd forgotten about that. But John's attitude was a bit of a worry.

"John, if word gets out we were taking the pish out of the paramilitaries we'll be fuckin' girders somewhere. And another thing, Carol must never, ever, get wind of this. We know the prick deserved what came to him, but she wouldnae appreciate the gesture. And one final, final thing. You don't owe Carol anything anymore. You're even. Stay away from her, understand? "

John took a final draw on his joint and stubbed it out on the sole of one of his trainers.

"Right on Jim ma man."

He put the roach away in his tracksuit pocket.

"Funny as fuck but, wintit?"

* * *

A few hours later, back at Jim's place, John was paid off and was away to score with the hundred quid Jim gave him. He looked like a wee boy that'd been given some pennies for sweeties.

Jim went into the kitchen to get another can and turn on the immersion heater. He needed a bath. Then he was going up to see Josie. He'd been avoiding her for two days, trying to get ready for the Stranraer trip. As well as that, he just didnae know how to tell Josie about the Carol situation. He knew that Josie would totally nip his head about it: her and Carol were big buddies.

He had to keep telling himself he was doing the right thing. Carol was turning into his da, carping and criticising, wearing him out with disapproval. If it wisnae so painful it would be funny. All these years, he'd been worried that he was gonnae turn out like the old bastard, and then he starts to recognise the signs in the woman he loved. Loves still in fact, but that would fade away through time. It had to, he couldnae keep feeling like this forever.

No, he just had to keep avoiding her, and look for other distractions. Like Siobhan for instance. But she would have to wait until he got through the big pile of work he had in his holdall. Two more assignments and a final exam and if all went well he was off to Paisley Uni full time, for the last two years of the Honours Degree. No more working in the shop and then studying into the wee sma' hours. He couldnae wait to see Mick and Josie's face: he never tellt anybody he was a part time student in case he failed again, became a two-time drop out.

He was mostly looking forward to seeing Frew's face: he couldnae wait to tell him to stick his job up his arse. He'd have to live on student loans for a while, but he'd get a job easy enough, pay them off in no time. There were always vacancies for Systems Analysts. He could go to America, take Josie and the wean with him. She'd wanted to go there with that waster Rab after all.

He caught sight of his arms as he opened the fridge door. Totally scratched to fuck from hanging about in bushes to make sure Boyle made it out of the van. It had looked for a minute that he was stuck in there, even tho' they'd left the doors open for him. John was all for going back in, but Jim had held him back. Not after what they'd seen and heard in that close.

He smiled to himself. If that prick Boyle had pulled his hood off, they would've had to kill him. It would've been too much of a red neck to try to convince him that John was a loyalist hit man, even an apprentice one. Wee John, the pygmy paramilitary, not even the size of a decent shite.

Twenty-one

Fucking yes! John was right up there. He'd used some of his wages to buy a baggie of sulph. He was gonnae share it with Div, if he could find him. They could go clubbing, blow the whole wad. It wisnae often he'd a hundred quid to burn.

He was halfway up Div's street when he heard a screech and a car horn. Right behind him, for fuck's sake. He nearly jumped out of his skin.

"How you doin', wee man?"

It was Div, hanging out of a red Vauxhall Astra, grinning like a fucking skull.

"Heh, I nearly shat masel' there! Where'd you get the motor?"

"Up the toon. Want a ride?"

"Where to?"

"Dunno. You comin' or whit?"

John got in the motor. The bottom bit of the dashboard was ripped out, no keys in the ignition.

"Whit you been up to Johnnie Boy? No' seen you in ages."

"I was daein' a job for a pal of mine."

"Whit type of job?"

"Never mind. Got well paid tho'. And I've got some of this."

John pulled out the baggie from his pocket. Div's eyes lit up.

"Well done wee man. See us some of that."

Div ripped open the packet with his spare hand and snorted straight out of the bag. He leaned back in his seat, both hands behind his head. John had to grab the steering wheel, before they wrapped themselves round a lamppost.

"Fuck sake Div, get a grip!"

Div's eyes were watering as he passed the bag back to John.

"This is good stuff, wee man, my fuckin' heart's turning somersaults already! You no' having any yoursel'?"

"If I could get near it, ya maddie!"

John took a snort of the whizz and finished it off. His cousin was right, this stuff was pure berries. His heart was racing, he couldnae keep still, he wanted to run about inside the car.

"Get some sounds on, wee man"

John pressed play on the CD player. Right away the car was flooded with the thrash of electric guitars and heavy drums. Thump, thump. He could feel the music before he could hear it.

"Who the fuck's that?"

John looked at the CD case lying at his feet. A bunch of scary looking guys, masks on. Daft cunts. Tourists. They should try walking through Brigton Cross at midnight.

"Slipknot."

"Slipknot! Aw, no. This car must belong to some student wanker. Get somethin' else!"

"Cannae find anythin' else."

"Well turn the volume up then!"

John turned the dial full tilt. The whole car was booming, like one big amp. He couldnae make out the words – something like rar, rar, rar. His ears were ringing. He was going deaf. Fucking brilliant!

Div pressed hard on the accelerator. Flashlights were popping all over the place, as they set off every speed camera in their path. Gonnae cost that student a fortune.

He knew where they were going. Southside. Pollokshields. Long, straight roads. He and Div had managed a ton once, right over a hill. For a wee second, he'd had a feeling of weightlessness, the nearest he would ever get to being one of thae astronauts. They both stoated their heids off the roof. Excellent! Whiplash an' everything.

That motor didnae have a sunroof. This one did. He wound back the glass and started climbing through it.

Heh, whit you daein'?"

"I'm gonnae ride on the roof."

"Don't be fuckin' dense. Sit doon."

Div grabbed his waistband, and pulled his trackies down. He'd no kegs on.

"Heh, leave's alane, ya poof. Are you tryin' to gies a blow job?"

He was halfway through. He sat his arse down, and wedged himself in by his knees. He spread his arms wide. It started to rain. Chucking it down. His trackie top was soaked. He lost his cap. The rain was pelting off him. The car was weaving all ower the joint. He kept getting smacked in the face with bits of wet trees. Overhanging branches. He was fucking freezing. Fucking buzzing. Top of the world man.

Div turned a corner on two wheels. John could see the pavement coming towards him. When the motor straightened, he fell back inside. His trousers were still halfway down. He'd a bother pulling the waistband over his boner.

"You'll no' get rid of that for hours, wee man. Better find a burd."

The CD was still playing. He could make out the words now:

Only one of us walks away
Only one of us walks away

They both took up the chant, screaming at the top of their voices, trying to outdo the stereo.

Then Div turned the volume down.

"I tell you what, wee man. Is it no' time you dug up that cunt that landed you in the hospital?"

John had forgot all about him. That many things had happened since.

"I'm no' bothered."

"No bothered! You're a fuckin' shitebag, you mean."

Div swerved to avoid a fanny on a bike. Just saw him at the last minute. John looked in the rear mirror, in time to see the guy come flying off and land on a hedge. He'd on a helmet 'tho.

"We've gottae dump this motor soon, Div, we're gonnae get lifted."

"Don't try to change the subject. Shitebag."

John had promised Jim he would never tell about the trip to Stranraer. That would prove he wisnae a shitebag! But he'd given his word. It was his bond.

"She still fancies you, you know."

"Who?"

"His burd. The one you shagged. Whit was her name?"

"Lee Anne. How d'you know if she still fancies me? She's never been in touch."

"She's too feart of him. Frightened she gets another doin'."

"A doin'?"

"Aye. He punched her lights out after he'd finished with you. Did you no' know?"

"The dirty bastard."

"Aye, in front of their wean, I heard. Broken cheekbone."

He knew what he should do. The same as Jim. Claim the cunt.

"She likes you, you know. You could be right in there, if you got rid of him. She's got her own hoose an' everythin'. Sky telly."

It was still Valentine's Day.

"Right. Let's go and find him."

He was easy to find. Every night, he sat for a while under the Umbrella, at Brigton Cross. Him and his pals played at terrorising the jaikies. They parked the motor at the shops and waited. Twenty minutes later, there they were. Three of them. Easy.

They got out of the motor. Div pulled down the zip of his jacket.

"You tooled up?"

"Naw. Just gettin' comfy."

The two of them wandered over to the Umbrella. Dead casual. The guy they were looking for was squeezing one of the jaikey's faces, kidding on he was kidding like. The jaikey's taped up specs were hanging off his face, and he was trying to laugh. John knew the wee guy. Malky. Couldnae talk right. Stuttered.

John walked right up to them.

"Heh you. Big fuckin' hard man. Leave him alane!"

And he did. He flung Malky to one side. He just stood there, staring. In fact everybody was staring. Even the traffic noises seemed to stop. Finally the guy piped up.

"You talkin' to me, ya wee prick?"

"Aye, I fuckin' am!"

"Good. I've been lookin' for you for months. I see you were shacked up wi' your boyfriend there. D'you think you'll be third time lucky, wee man?"

The guy came towards him but John stood his ground. John ducked as he took a swing at him and punched the guy in the balls. That was for Lee Anne. The guy doubled over, fell to the ground. John felt a bit disappointed. Was that it? But he'd forgotten about the two pals. He felt a dunt and heard a smashing noise. Somebody'd hit him over the heid with a bottle. He fell down. Then they were on him. Fut! His belly. Fut! Another one. Kidneys. He tried to get up and got kicked in the jaw.

They were taking it slow. Not like the last time, when Jim was there. But where was Div?

He looked through their legs and saw Div, still staring.

Bang. From the flashes of light he'd guess his nose was broken. He covered his face, rolled on to his back. Somebody kicked him in the ribs. Snap. Somebody else stamped on his balls. Funny thing – he didnae feel any pain. Yet.

Then he saw wheels. Wee feet. He looked up, there was a wean in a buggy, looking at him. Then Lee Anne.

"Heh, darlin', remember this wee fucker?"

She glanced at him, shrugged and turned the pushchair round.

"Was that the one that got me drunk last summer? Tried to rape me?"

Was he hearing straight? Rape her? She'd been all over him like fucking flea bites. He caught her eye for a split second. She was scared. Selling him out to save herself. Could he blame her but?

"Heh boys, check this out. Cunt's got a hard on. Dirty rapist bastard!"

"Get his troosers aff him."

Somebody yanked at his trackies, pulled them down to his ankles.

"Nnnnnow. D'you nnnnot think he'sss had enough?" stuttered Malky, the homeless guy.

"Fuck off. Windae licker. You wantin' to be next?"

A broken bottle was waved in front of his face.

"D'you know what should happen to rapists an' perverts like you?"

No! They couldnae do that! One of them pulled his trackies over his ankles, to spread his legs. He tried to get up, but somebody was leaning on his shoulders. He could see Lee Anne in the distance. Was she on her mobile? Nobody else seemed to notice her.

He opened his mouth to scream but nothing came out. His lips moved. Jim. But Jim wisnae here.

Lee Anne's man knelt down between his legs. He was holding a broken bottle.

"I'm gonnae cut it off, wee man. No more nookie for you."

He found enough strength from somewhere to twist round, looking for his cousin. He saw him, standing behind the others, greetin'. He screwed his eyes shut and waited. Only one of us walks away. And it wisnae gonnae be him. Then he heard a crack, like a whip, and a heavy weight crashed on him, pinning him down. He was gonnae be sick. Something warm and wet was dripping on his face.

He opened his eyes. Right above him was a checked shirt, missing a button. Blood was seeping through it. He turned his face away and saw Div, holding a gun.

Lee Anne's man was still breathing, but he sounded like he was making a dirty phone call. It nearly drowned out the noise of the sirens.

Twenty-two

Josie laughed softly to herself. Sarah's head was lying against the side of the chair, with a little bit of spittle rolling down her chin. She'd be mortified if she knew.

She'd told Sarah to take it easy, but she refused, although she looked completely knackered. Kathleen was six weeks old now, and Sarah had been up to visit Josie nearly every morning, accompanied either by a bag of messages, or more baby clothes. Josie tried to look grateful and pleased at the completely impractical outfits, typical doting granny stuff: tiny satin and lace dresses, far too expensive, only going to last a few weeks, and murder to get on and off when Kathleen puked all over them.

"Look, Sarah, this must be costing you something terrible." Josie held up a tiny silky jacket, emblazoned with a bunny. "She's got enough for the time being ..."

"Och, I know that Josie. I'll calm down eventually. I'm just all taken with my wee sweetheart there. Anywise, it's nae bother, honest. I've been paying into a club in the baby shop in Brigton Cross for months. Here, I've bought you a chocolate Easter egg. Don't gimme ony nonsense about diets when you're feeding the wean yourself ..."

She'd sat down, took one look over at Kathleen in her Moses basket and then fell fast asleep.

Josie couldn't sleep. She had to watch her child constantly, in case something happened to her the minute she looked away. She knew it was irrational and post-baby madness, but she couldn't help herself. Kathleen wriggled about in the basket. What a funny face she was pulling! She put her tiny hands up to her face and pulled at the skin round her eyes. It was a completely random act, but Josie lifted her up, in case she harmed herself.

Maybe she was hungry. Josie had gone to breast-feeding workshops but it was nothing like the real thing. Bring the baby to you. Nipple to chin. That'll make the baby want to suckle. Then make sure the baby is fully latched on: the nipple should be well back in the baby's mouth. Unfortunately, Kathleen had been in the womb at the time, so she hadn't been paying attention.

It was terrible in the hospital. Every time Josie presented her nipple, Kathleen let it fall out of her mouth. Josie's breasts had become engorged: if she couldn't feed Kathleen she was going to burst. But the longer she left it, the more difficult it was for the baby to latch on. To her little mouth, it was like trying to swallow a huge lemon. Shortly to become a melon.

Then one time the nipple stayed in, and the little jaws clamped down over it. Josie had watched Kathleen's facial muscles, sucking away, drawing in nourishment from her mother. She'd felt a wave of love wash over her, so physical that she knew her flow had increased: she could feel her milk draining away, her breasts reducing, losing their hardness.

They'd both got the hang of it now, and Josie was more relaxed in her own home, propped up in the chair with cushions. She lifted her top and loosened her nursing bra. The baby, smelling the milk, nuzzled in. *Kathleen. Katie. Katie Kitten. Little rabbit.* Josie murmured all these endearments to her wee baby daughter, who just sucked away, oblivious to everything.

When she was training to be a teacher, one lecturer tried to tell them what it felt like to be a parent: that the world was divided into those with children and those without, and now she knew what he was talking about. Now there was always going to be someone else to consider, whose needs went before hers, whose pain would be her pain. Josie had lost control of her Universe. Her happiness now relied solely on the well-being of her child.

Her nipples were still tender, the earlier failed attempts to breast-feed had burst and peeled the skin. They were better now but still sore. She didn't care. She'd do anything for this wee scrap of life. Josie now understood what real love was: the love for a child, totally unconditional and absolute.

She'd thought about Rob a lot since his daughter was born. She'd never loved Rob like this. She'd wanted him, and would never have given him up, even though in her heart she knew he wasn't that happy being with her. The look of love was never in his eyes.

Nobody was to blame for that; it was just how it was. There had been no real barriers to their loving each other; even the religion thing wasn't that much of a big deal, when it came down to it. His mother wasn't that bad, a bit of a Hun, but bearable. No, it was just that Rob's heart belonged to another. If she was really honest, she knew by the look on his face when she told him she was pregnant. She knew there and then that there was someone else. That's why Michael's mad idea of communal confession had terrified her: she didn't want to know Rob's secrets.

Sarah started coughing. Mother of God, she'd nearly told her all about Michael. What good would that have done? Michael, her big brother, born between her and Jim, but to a different mother. Same father. His uncle.

Auntie Bridget had come to live with them not long after Josie was born. Granny McDaid had died and her wee flat was to be sold. It was only a room and kitchen in Govanhill, and gran and papa, when he was alive, had slept in the kitchen. When they were growing up, Bridget and her big brother had slept in the front room, in the fold down couch.

Bridget was probably the only woman her da had ever loved, or what passed for love in his mind. Josie could still remember them together when she was a wee girl. The way he spoke to her, opened doors for her, carried bags for her. He'd treated his own wife with disdain, as if she was in the way.

But Bridget wasn't a happy woman. The car driver had said she came out of nowhere, jumped right out in front of him. He'd no chance to stop in time, it was a dual carriageway, and he'd been driving at the speed limit. He didn't even see her until she came through the windscreen. She was miles from home, or her usual route to her work.

Their da was inconsolable. He'd sat with the open coffin in the front room for two whole days and nights. Both Father Leary and the Undertaker had advised a covered coffin but he was hearing none of it. As they were getting ready to bring the body to the Chapel he snatched her up, cradling her smashed head in his arms and wouldn't let anyone near her, or him. Michael and Josie were screaming. Jim and Kathleen were trying to get them out of the room. In the end their da had missed the funeral, locked up in a room in the Chapel House, under Father Leary's instructions.

He never recovered. His bullying went from browbeating and contempt to violent rages. Jim and Kathleen suffered the most. Josie knew how to keep out of the way, but Jim always tried to rescue his mother from the blows, only making their da worse. Poor Michael escaped his wrath, in fact was his favourite, the object of his affections. But that only made the unlucky boy more miserable than the rest of them put together.

Baby Kathleen would learn none of this. He

would never get near this wee one. If he ever tried to even enter the same room as her daughter, Josie knew she would kill him.

But what family would wee Kathleen have round her as she was growing up? Her two uncles, her mammy and her other grandparents, or a granny at least. The Dan one had still to come round. Still, she could live without him as well. Another old git.

Twenty-three

He could see the bus stop from the window, but there was no way he wanted her to catch him keeking out from behind the curtains like a right 'jessie'.

It was the afternoon but it was dreich and dreary outside. He opened the curtains wide and sat at the table by the window. This way he'd still see her get off the bus, but she wouldnae see him.

Things werenae right between them. They were still talking, but no' the way it should be. What had happened to women nowadays? When he was growing up in Brigton, wives did what they were tellt. He couldnae see his mother traipsing round, flouting his da's wishes. Sarah was doing it to provoke him.

He was gasping for a fag, but the room was so dull she might see the glow from up the street. Maybe if he cupped it in his hand, the way his faither did? Out of the blue, he had a memory of his da doling out a skite for getting a hole in his breeks or whatever. A great muckle hand landing on the side of his head, knocking him sideways into the dresser. That would be followed swiftly with another one for tipping over his mammy's vase. The hand had seemed to come out of the sky, and didnae seem to belong to onybody. But he knew it was his da because of the nicotine stain in the palm.

His jacket was over the back of the chair. He reached into a pocket and got out his fags and matches. There was an ashtray on the table already, but it had wee bits of wood shavings in it. Smellt flowery. One of Sarah's ideas – "pot pourri". When she first bought the stuff he'd joked to her that there'd be no 'popery' in his house. She laughed. But that was before the boy had died.

He reached into another pocket and brought out his paper. He spread it on the table and tipped the wood shavings on to it. She could put them back in herself if she was that keen. Ashtrays were to keep douts and ash in, no' to make the room smell like a boudoir.

He lit up, took a long draw then turned the fag round so that the tip was hid in his hand. There was a bit of light coming in off the street, so he could make out the headline in his paper: 'MSP in Adultery Divorce Shame'.

Every other day there was something like this in the news. Judgement Day was coming, there was nothing surer. He didnae know exactly when – it was only thae sad weirdoes in cults that tried to second guess God's Will, with their mass suicides that were guaranteeing their place in Hell – but he felt it more strongly every day, it would soon be time to stand up and be counted.

It used to be that he was ready to meet his God, but lately he'd been worried about Sarah.

She was a good, kind woman, a bit keen on fripperies, but a good Protestant woman, a defender of the reformed faith. But it was her kindness that was getting her into danger, feeling sorry for that female. An unnatural family. They'd reached out and poisoned the boy. Now they were trying to get at his mother.

He'd tried to tell her but he couldnae say the words. He'd pollute their air. She used to aye know what he was thinking. How come she'd lost her gift? Brainwashed by that Papist mob.

She kept insisting that wean was their flesh and blood, because the wee strumpet said so. But Dan knew otherwise. He'd tried to let on what he knew. The Bible open on the table, a marker under the passage – Corinthians 6:9. She didnae even read it, just closed it and put it away in the drawer.

The boy. He was fine when he was wee. Studious. Nothing wrong with that. But as a young man? He was foolish, headstrong and refused to join the Lodge.

'He had the right to his own opinions.'

The fag burnt down over an inch. Dan watched as the ash tipped over his shirt cuff.

Well, "his own opinions" had got him in tow with yon McDaid tribe, corrupted by lust.

Dan stubbed out his fag in the ashtray. He leant over the table, his head in both his hands. He knew he was greetin', but he couldnae help it. He wiped his nose on his sleeve, felt the ash mix with his snot and be smeared across his cheek. Blubbering like a 'jessie' and with a mawkit face. He went through to the bathroom. She couldnae see him like this. He didnae bother with the light, just sined his face in the darkness.

That last day, the boy had been waiting for his mother to come home, but Sarah was making tea and sandwiches in the Orange Halls. Dan had nipped away to change his shirt and have a wash.

He'd called it love. He'd asked Dan to break the news to his mother. He couldnae believe it, but when the boy insisted, had even laughed at Dan's disgust, he thought his heart would burst. Dan tried to warn him that a life of sin and debauchery meant not only would he be turning his back on his family and his community, but risking his very soul. Dan had even quoted the scriptures to him:

"Know you not that the unrighteous shall not inherit the kingdom of God? Be you not deceived: neither fornicators, nor idolaters, not adulterers ... shall inherit the kingdom of God ... but you are sanctified, but you are justified in the name of the Lord Jesus, and by the spirit of our God."

The boy became enraged then, but it was guilt that fed Robert's anger, his one saving grace. He'd spat at Dan and stormed out of the house.

The burning lump was in his throat again. He'd failed the boy, and now he was dead. Murdered.

Dan was an old man now. Tired and weary. Ready to go when called. But could he thole an eternity without his son?

The front door opened. She'd got off the bus while he was in blubbering over the sink. He washed his face again. He could hear her moving about ben the kitchen. He went through. Her back was to him as he put a tumbler to the tap.

"Well?"

"Well whit?"

"Are you no' going to ask me where I've been?"

She was putting her messages in the fridge, refusing to look at him.

"Why should I?"

Sarah sighed, her head down.

"Why're you so hard Dan? You never used to be like this."

"I'm no' changed. It's you that's goin' off your nut, chasing after that wee hoor whenever she clicks her fingers."

Sarah closed the fridge door, still not looking at him. She took the tumbler out of his hand and put it on the drainer.

"You've had your say. Listen to me now. If you ever miscall that lassie again, either to my face or behind my back, I'm packing my bags and I'm out of here. For goodness sake's, she's just had our grandwean! I'll never turn my back on them."

Dan felt his stomach turn over. He stared at her.

"And don't gie me that look. I'm deadly serious."

He pushed by her, out of the kitchen. If she left he was finished. He had a sudden vision of that poor bugger Archie Reid. A pitiful state to get into. But then again it was always the drink with Reid, never his family.

He went ben to the room and sat down in the darkness, until he could breathe right again.

He couldnae lose Sarah. He'd already lost his wee boy, through his own fault. In trying to turn him round he'd fired him up. Made him walk into that pub just out of spite against *him*. He probably wanted to give Dan a public showing up. Didnae quite understand whit reaction he'd provoke .

There were those who saw the day of the Walk as an excuse for drunkenness and rabble rousing. They were as bad as the Papists: they didnae fear God. Most of them had never been in a church in their life. It was one of that crew that had committed murder. So far they'd got away with it. But, we are a short time on this earth. There was an eternity of punishment waiting for them.

There would be punishment, but no comfort for Dan. His son was dead. If he was a Roman Catholic, Dan could pray on his knees to a plaster saint, to try to cut a deal for the boy, so that he might be allowed to enter God's kingdom. But he was a Presbyterian. He knew there were no deals to be struck. Robert's doom was dealt. This was a terrible thing to know.

And now Sarah was threatening to leave him. He'd tried to protect her, and in doing so had turned her against him. Well, she would have to be tellt. Everything.

Twenty-four

Mick had one more exam to go and his finals would be over. He was expecting a First or an Upper Second at the very least. But it was a right pain in the arse having to study right through the whole Easter break.

All the other years him and Rab had just went up the Kelvingrove Park, if it was warm enough, to eye up all the lassies sitting in swotty wee groups with their lecture notes. Those memories made him want to laugh and cry at the same time.

He couldnae concentrate on his studies. He'd felt weird all day. Unsettled. There was a word for it, what was it? 'Portentous'. Maybe it was exam nerves. Maybe. He'd go and see Josie and the baby. He wanted any excuse to leave his bedsit, so he didnae phone ahead to find out if they were in. He could take a text book with him, try to read it on the subway over.

There was always hundreds of cars on Great Western Road, so when a Polis wagon put on its siren to jump the lights he took no notice at all. He'd stopped assuming they were after him.

The walk from Bridge Street subway to Josie's took him about ten minutes, just enough time to clear his head of Robotics and Simulation, Power System Design, Engineering Dynamics, and Condition Monitoring of Machinery. He was briefly free to think. A dangerous activity these days, he should've stayed at home with his books.

When he got to Josie's flat, there was no answer at first. Then who should answer the door but Sarah. When she clocked him standing there, he could tell by her face that something was up.

"Where's Josie?"

"Sleeping with the wean."

"Maybe I'll come back later then."

"Get into that living room! I want a word with you, out of earshot of that wee lassie."

As he went down the long hall he heard her softly close Josie's bedroom door.

He flung himself down on the couch, casually throwing his book onto the coffee table. "Advanced Computational Fluid Dynamics" by Professsor JS Weir, one of Michael's tutors.

"Any chance of a cuppa tea?"

He'd played this role so long now, he couldnae stop. The glaikit pal. The big galoot. Mad professor cousin and/or brother. Dead brainy but no common sense, aye coming away with crackers, saying the first thing that came into his head. But he never tellt them about his bad dreams.

She sat down opposite him.

"Right, what have you got to say for yourself? Now, don't act the innocent. I know all about you and Robbie."

"What are you talking about, missus?"

Gie in, gie in. Why keep this going?

"You and him. You two, you were ... *going with*

256

each other!"

She'd leaned right over to him, was whispering the words, too ashamed to say them outright. Her face was inches from his. She'd the same mad eyes as Rab got from time to time.

"Going with each other? Like courting. Like an item?"

He was talking shite, to buy time.

"Do you know how obsessed he was about hiding everything from you? You'd turned him into a right mammy's boy, did you know that missus?"

"Nonsense! It was *you* that turned him into a ... gay boy, a queer."

He laughed sardonically.

"It's no' quite as easy as that. Rab wisnae gay."

She passed her hands over her face, shook her head.

"Och, I'm no' getting this at all! Whit d'you mean, he wisnae gay? He was carrying on with you!"

Her confusion made him want to be cruel.

"He shagged girls sometimes. So what? I've shagged a few myself, out of curiosity. But the truth was he *made love* to me, and I *made love* to him. Are you listening Missus? Your precious wee boy was a man who enjoyed having sex with another man. That was the only time in his life he was really honest with himself. But he couldnae cope with the truth - you'd made him too full of hang ups. He didnae want to see himself as a 'gay boy' or a 'poof'."

"Aye, he had wanted to be normal, that's why he started going out with a lassie."

She'd never get it. She was too old. Too set in her puritanical ways.

"Sarah. Believe me. There's no such thing as normal."

"Ach, away with you! Is that what a University education teaches you?"

"I learnt all I needed to know about life long before I went to Uni. My upbringing taught me what big fuckin' lies most of us are living."

"Yourself included. What about Josie? You were brought up with her. Is she living a lie?"

"Of course she is. Look around you at this house. She was a student living in the middle of the fuckin' Gorbals an' she tried to make this place look like something from the Modern Homes Exhibition. All she needed was a nice man with prospects to make her wee world perfect."

"Here you!"

She stood over him, her voice shrill.

"That's your family you're talking about. You were deceiving her, chasing her man behind her back. You're no' human."

"Josie wouldnae let him go. He was on the brink of chuckin' her a dozen times, but he couldnae hurt her feelings."

She was sitting down again, her face as white as a sheet.

"You've got no shame, have you?"

He wanted her to hate him. He didnae want to be understood or be forgiven. He didnae deserve it.

"Don't get me wrong. Of course I felt a wee bit rotten. If it wisnae for me she might have met some nice Catholic headmaster and lived happily ever after. It was me that introduced Josie to your fucked up son."

"Don't call him that! You're not fit enough to lick his boots!"

"I'm only tellin' you the truth Sarah."

She stared at him for ages. He tried to stare back but she could see right through him.

And then she came right out with it.

"If you loved him why did you kill him?"

Relief flooded through him. Thank Christ. It was over.

"Did you know he told his daddy all about you? He was gonnae leave Josie and go and live with you?"

A cold chill went right through him. Rab was dancin' on his grave.

Then she laughed at him. Rab had laughed the same, that last night.

"You never knew that, did you? He never tellt you his plans. What have you been thinkin' all this time? That he picked Josie o'er you? I hate to tell you, but you won him in the end."

He couldnae speak. He was trying to take it all in. The enormity of what Sarah was saying to him.

"And you just left him there. He wanted to

spend his life with you, and you left him to die."

He stood up. He knew where he was going. It was just as he headed for the hallway, that he saw Josie standing behind the living room door. How much had she heard? It didnae matter but. It would be easier for her later if she hated him.

"Michael. Wait!"

But he pushed past her, up the hall and nearly out the door. The old woman shouted after him.

"The Police will be here ony minute now. I've already phoned them!"

If they were looking for him, he'd better hurry up.

* * *

The River Clyde was in full spate. Good old equinoctial gales. Or it might have been the global warming. Anyway, the cause didnae matter. All that mattered to Mick was that he couldnae swim.

The parapet of King's Bridge was waist high, so it was nothing for him to straddle it, ready to throw himself in. He was going to join Rab, wherever he was.

He hadnae meant to kill him, he was just raging at him for getting his wee sister pregnant. That last night, she was so happy when she told him about the baby.

He went looking for Rab then, to have it out with him. He was on the same street when Rab burst out of that pub like the fuckin' Pied Piper. Mick had followed him to save him from the Huns that were baying for his blood. But when he saw

260

him on the bridge, puking his guts up, he thought he was drunk, that he'd been celebrating becoming a daddy. Mick had been disgusted at his hypocrisy. Rab was acting the big man, but not big enough to admit who he really was.

He'd re-run those last moments in his head a thousand times in the last eight months, trying to think of it as a freak accident. He'd only lashed out the once. One kick, that was all. He'd got worse than that at the Judo. And that wisnae what killed him. It was the vomit, in the end. Mick had just kicked him once, turned and walked away, intending to get out of Rab and Josie's life for ever. No looking back, all he'd meant to do was reclaim his pride.

One kick. It had taken him all of two seconds to deliver it. In two seconds he'd stolen a life. Stained with his lover's blood, he wisnae a man anymore, he was a murderer. But he'd finally become a monster when he decided he could maybe get away with it. Fuck. He could've given Rab lessons in the art of hypocrisy. Two lives were finished that night. It had just taken Mick longer to die, but he was putting an end to it now. No more deceit. No more studying to block it all out, kidding himself on that he still had a future, that he could get a good job and make it up to Josie and the wean, somehow. He was getting what he deserved.

He jumped.

The freezing water was like a punch in the guts.

He sank down, but his lungs were still full of air, and he floated back to the top. His coat was spread out around him like a cloud, keeping him buoyant. He should've put stones in his pockets. He struggled out of his coat and dived under. He tried to empty his lungs, but all his instincts were trying to save him, and he kept floating to the top. Every time his head went above water, he gulped in air, despite himself.

Then he felt his strength leaving him, he was gradually sinking to the murky bottom, to become food for the river rats. He felt the weeds on the river-bed wrap themselves around his legs, keeping him at the bottom. The water was filthy. But why should that that worry him now? He was losing consciousness, finally getting away. Then he sensed movement round about him, a confusion of bubbles, arms round his middle, pulling him up to the surface. No! He thrashed about. He managed to get his fingers wrapped round the guy's hair, and pulled him back down with him. But they surfaced again.

"Mick, for fuck's sake. Are you gonnae kill me too?"

Jim. His big brother, still looking after him. He let him drag him to the bank, somehow. Hands were hauling him out, and somebody was pumping his arms, forcing the foul water out of his lungs. He was a failure. Couldnae even drown himself.

He opened his eyes, and looked up, saw figures

crowded round him. There was Josie trying to get at him, but being held back by the Polis. She was probably trying to throw him back in. He was gonnae pass out again, but just before he did, he could have sworn he heard her voice:

"Michael. I'm sorry. Forgive me."

Twenty-five

Archie had his good suit on. The rest of his clothes were spread out on the couch, being separated into the 'straight for the bin' pile, and the 'will do him for now, but throw them out as soon as they get dirty, they're not worth the cost of the laundrette' pile.

His name had finally got to the top of the list. He was going to the Landressy Street Home for the Elderly that very afternoon. The place had been custom built on a gap site, and looked like a bright and modern hotel. He would have his own room and bathroom, but with round-the-clock care and a communal lounge and dining room.

"D'you know, Carol, I didnae even know this place existed until a few months ago. I just hope the Tam one stays away."

"He'll never be allowed in, the staff will get him jailed if he even tries. Anyway, according to the Community Police, he's disappeared off the face of the planet. Even his poor ex-wife hasn't heard from him in weeks."

"He's another bugger I wish had fell in the river and drowned."

Annie completely disapproved of Michael's rescue, thought it was all staged to get him some sympathy from the Jury. He was still on Suicide Watch in Barlinnie Prison, awaiting trial for Culpable Homicide. Carol had pulled a few strings, and managed to find out that he intended to plead guilty.

Annie held up a pair of grubby grey pants.

"Let's no' even bother checking his underwear. I'll go to Littlewoods before closing and buy him a few new sets."

"Fine, I'll give you the money. In fact mum, can we just apply that principle to the rest of his gear? There's nothing worth keeping really. The poly-bags are worth more than the clothes."

Annie flung the remaining clothes into a black bin bag, and made a space for herself on the couch.

"You're absolutely right, pet. When I think what a dandy your dad was in his day! A new safari suit every summer, whether we'd the money or not. Anyway, away through and put the kettle on and make a pot of tea. Make him a wee piece n' butter. He's had nothing to eat since half seven this morning."

It was when she was looking for clean cups in the kitchen that she heard Annie call out to her:

"And now that your daddy's settled, we can talk about your future."

So typical of her mother, straight to the point, although Carol was surprised that she'd waited until she was out of the room. Not like Annie to be backward at coming forward.

Carol poured the tea and arranged a plate of buttered bread on a tray for Archie. She gently kicked the living room door open, as her hands were full.

"There's nothing to discuss mum, it's over. I visited him once in the hospital, to see if he was OK, and that was the last time I saw him. "

"And do you plan to see him in the future?"

"I very much doubt it. Can we change the subject, mum?"

Carol's voice was catching in her throat. Archie looked up at her, bewildered, still chewing on his piece. He put his cup down on the tray on his lap, patted her hand and gave it a slobbery kiss, leaving a little circle of breadcrumbs. He kept hold of her, while staring accusingly over at Annie, silently blaming her for Carol's upset.

"It's OK, dad, we're just talking about something. I need to go to the toilet. Could you gimme my hand back, please?"

In the bathroom, she splunged her face with cold water, and was reaching out for the towel when it was put into her hands by Annie.

"Carol, pet, I didnae meant to get you all agitated. I know I'm a nosy old bag. It's just that I worry about you. You're still my wee lassie."

Annie put the toilet lid down, spread loo roll over the surface, and sat Carol down on it. She settled herself on the edge of the bath, then handed Carol another few sheets from the roll.

"Here pet, blow your nose."

Carol took the paper and blew. It was the cheap stuff, rough as a badger's bum.

"Look mum, there's no point in talking about

him. It's over."

"Aye well, as long as it stays that way. You'll meet a nice man eventually. Just do what it says in the problem pages – get out of the house, join a club, do voluntary work. That's what I did."

It took a few seconds for Carol to realise what Annie was saying to her.

"Mum! You've got a boyfriend?"

"I certainly do not have a boyfriend!"

"Well, what do you have then?"

"A gentleman friend; who is also my fiancé."

"A fiancé! Bloody hell, is there no end to your talents! How come you never told me about him before?"

"Well, initially I felt rotten telling you about my second man, when you couldnae even get a first."

Good old Annie, a comfort to the last.

"Then you were running about with the Jim one, and I didnae want you and him giving me a showing up. But now you're single again I cannae keep Alistair hidden away forever."

She should work for the Samaritans.

"So tell me all about him. Where did you meet him, what does Alistair do for a living, has he got a bought house?"

"In the Barnardo's Charity Shop in Rutherglen. He volunteers the same days as me. He's a retired accountant. And yes lady, he *has* got a big house in Burnside. Never been married, so no pesky grown up children to accuse me of cheating them out of their inheritance."

"Mother you're such an operator! But do you love him?"

Annie stared speculatively at the tiles on the wall opposite.

"He's a tee-totaller, never went out much when he was young. A bit shy, too. He didnae have your daddy's Dutch courage with the drink. That's how he never met anybody. But I'm bringing him out of his shell. I've got him going to the line dancing two nights a week."

"You never answered my question, mum. Do you love him?"

"He's a gentleman and I'm very fond of him. That'll do for now. He's good company, but we don't have years in front of us, so it would be daft to get to the stage where we couldnae live without each other. I'm too old for all that ecstasy and I've already had the agony with Archie."

Carol stood up and cuddled her mother.

"I'm pleased for you mum. You deserve a bit if happiness."

"Thanks pet. I can be happy, now that your daddy's all sorted. I'm still fond of him, in my own way. But I've always wanted someone like Alistair. He's one of the good guys."

Twenty-six

Sarah heard Dan come up the stairs. She could aye tell his footsteps, firm and steady, never hesitating 'til he got to the front door, then two wipes of his shoes on the mat. When he was working she'd turn up the gas under the tatties as soon as she heard the first step. She had it timed so that his dinner would be on the table the minute he was washed and changed.

"Right Josie, that's him. You and the wean get into the front room."

The lassie looked doubtful.

"I'm doing this for you, Sarah. The slightest trouble and we're out of here."

"And I'll be at your back. Don't worry pet, he's no' that bad."

No sooner had she closed the door to the front room than Dan was standing in the lobby.

"Aye," he said as she took his jacket and bunnet off him. She didnae want him going into the press.

"Aye," she replied.

He kept looking at her. Could he tell she was a bag of nerves?

"Whit's for the tea?"

"Roast lamb."

He raised his eyebrows as he sat at the kitchen table.

"It's cheaper at this time of year."

He nodded and spread his paper on the table.

"Onyway. I thought we'd splash out. We've got visitors."

He looked up.

"Who you expectin'?"

"They're here already. In the front room."

"Who?"

"Josie. And the wean. The grandwean."

He said nothing, just stood up and made for the lobby. He opened the door to the front room. Josie was sitting on the settee, cuddling wee Kathleen to her. They both had their jackets on. Josie had Kathleen's travel bag over her shoulder.

He stared right past them.

"Out."

Josie stood up and looked at Sarah, 'I told you so' written all over her face.

"I'm going, but I need my pram."

"Whit?"

"Sarah put the pram in the hall cupboard. You're blocking the way."

"I'll move. You just take whit's yours and leave."

"Oh I will. Don't you worry."

Sarah should have known this was gonnae happen. Well, she wisnae havin this situation a second longer. She pushed by her man and stood in the centre of the room

"Josie. Sit down and don't say another word. Dan, take a seat."

"Sarah, are you off your head? I'm no' sittin' in

the same room as one of them."

He looked at her, heartbroken.

"They killed our boy, have you forgot that?"

Where was she to start?

"Dan. The one that killed our boy is in the jail. And even then, he says it was an accident. Whether it was or no', Josie didnae have a hand in it."

"How do you know she didnae entice Robert into their perverted world?"

Josie was on her feet, her face scarlet and her eyes brimming over.

"I don't have to listen to this."

Sarah was fed up with the both of them.

"Josie, aye you do! We're gonnae get this cleared up once and for all. Sit down and don't get upset. He doesnae know what he's saying."

"Oh aye I do. Get that lassie and her wean out of this house Sarah. And don't ever bring her back."

"If you send her away now I'm getting the cases from the top of the wardrobe and I'm going wi' her!"

That silenced him for a second. He sat down then.

"So, after all these years you take the side of strangers against your husband."

"Dan. After all these years you're still a stubborn old fool. It's no' a question of taking sides. Robbie's dead. Nobody in this room is responsible for that. Or maybe we're all responsible ..."

"Shite."

"Oh is it? Who sent him away that night? You. And what about me? I brought him up, cared for him every day and I never once guessed he was how he was. Josie never had a clue either, shared a bed with him and still never had a clue."

"Don't bring filthy talk into this house, woman."

"I'm not being filthy Dan. There's plenty of mention of men and woman lying wi' each other in the Bible. Are you saying that's filthy?"

"Blasphemy now! You're no' the woman I married."

"You're right. I'm forty years older and feeling it."

Sarah walked over to Josie.

"Let me have the wean for a minute."

Josie's eyes widened. She pulled the baby closer to her.

"No way. I'm not trusting him near my daughter."

"He's her grandfather. He'll no' harm her. Just for a wee second Josie. I'll no' let go of her, honest."

Josie loosened her grip of Kathleen. But when Sarah carried her over to Dan's chair Josie was on her feet, hovering a few inches behind her.

"Look Dan. Look at this wee innocent. She's our flesh and blood. If it wisnae for us, she wouldnae be here. She's got her mammy but she needs us as well."

Dan stared her straight in the face. He wouldn't

look down at the baby being held out to him.

"Sarah. Don't do this. Please."

"Take her Dan."

Sarah put Kathleen on his lap. Josie was over in a shot, ready to retrieve her wean. Sarah put an arm out to block her way.

"She'll be all right pet. Dan, look at her. Who's she the double of? Just look. Please. This is the last thing I'll ever ask of you."

Just then Kathleen squirmed, all the commotion bringing her out of her sleep. Instinctively, Dan held on to her, in case she fell. He couldnae help looking down. She'd stretched her wee tiny fists in the air and was yawning. Then she opened her eyes and looked straight at him. With that same quiet look on her face that Robbie often had.

Suddenly Josie swooped, grabbing her wean back.

Sarah sighed. It was hopeless.

"Can I go now Sarah?"

"You can Josie. I'll walk you down the road a bit. Get some fresh air."

She was getting her coat on when Dan appeared in the lobby.

"I'll help youse down wi' the pram."

It was a lovely evening outside. Very nearly summer.

Twenty-seven

Three Years Later

John was nearly hidden behind the large flat pack he was carrying.

"Where will I put this, Miss Reid?"

"Where did you find it?"

"The delivery guys gave me it at the bottom of the close."

"John – you should have made them bring it up the stairs to the office. Anyway, it's your desk. You're going into Patsy's room, so ask her where she wants it. You'll have to put it together yourself. There's a couple of screwdrivers lying around somewhere."

She'd agreed to take John on a work experience placement as part of his early release programme. He'd learned how to use a computer when he was in prison, and Patsy, God bless her, had finally agreed to try to train him in office skills. The government were giving them a grant to take him on, and Carol had bribed Patsy with the promise of a new IT system.

"Wait a minute John! It's Thursday – I thought this was your college day?"

"Disnae start 'til next week."

He was also down for an SVQ in Clerical Administration, much to the bemusement of Patsy, the most efficient legal secretary in the world, and without a qualification to her name.

"When you've finished with the desk, Patsy will show you where everything is and then you can go out and get the sandwiches and biccies for my lunchtime meeting."

"What, like a tea boy?"

"No, like the trainee. Do you think office work is all computers and filing? You're at the bottom of the pecking order, John, so you go the messages. Eventually, you can work your way up to answering the phones and stuff. When Patsy thinks you're ready."

"I'll have to go on the phones one day. Reception skills are part of my portfolio, y'know!"

Carol had managed to get his Attempted Murder charge down to Serious Assault. She'd persuaded the Procurator Fiscal that John was not 'art and part' to the shooting, in fact had no idea that his cousin had a gun. The judge had still sentenced him for six years, as an example to others. Nobody had believed the castration story, not even Carol. Eventually John had just stopped going on about it, got his head down and done his time quietly.

"John, you're out because of your so-called good behaviour, so away and behave, and let me get on with my work."

He went away in a huff. Patsy would soon have him tobered. What would Carol do without her? She had agreed to leave her steady job at FTQ and go with Carol, leaving a plush city centre office with all the latest technology, for a crummy office up a close in Rutherglen, with one ancient computer that crashed whenever the letter she was typing stretched to two pages. She'd even agreed to take a rent-free period in the flat, in lieu of wages, in the early days. Now that Carol's practice had built up, she had made Patsy part of a profit-sharing scheme, and had ordered a new computer network, complete with three terminals. They were installing the lot this afternoon, which was why John would have to get his desk put together this morning, unless he wanted to be practising his word processing sitting on the carpet.

* * *

The lunchtime meeting was a success. She'd managed to persuade a charity for women and children to put her on their list of legal representatives. Family Law; that was what she was into now, helping abused women squeeze some justice from an unfair world, and maybe even helping protect kids from the crazies who could do so much damage to their young lives and their future. She hoped to gradually move out of the criminal stuff, although for now it was paying the bills.

She was humming to herself as she tidied up the small meeting room, and was nearly singing when she carried the tray of crockery through reception to the kitchen area.

"Carol, you've finished your meeting early!"

This was more like an accusation from Patsy, rather than a statement of fact.

"Yes, the client had another meeting to go to, but I definitely think we've got an 'in' there, she just has to write a report for her Head Office in London, and we should be approved."

"Head Office, I thought she was the Chief Executive?"

"No, she's the Manager for Scotland. She's writing a report for the Board, Princess Anne or somebody's got to give us the nod ..."

"Great stuff. Why don't you get a bit of fresh air before the afternoon appointments? You're looking a bit peaky."

"I'm fine. I'll just open a window in my room. I enjoy that view of the bookie's car park anyway."

She breezed into her room, to find a pair of feet sticking out from her desk.

"D'you know Patsy, you'll need to be getting an electrician in here to rewire this place. This room disnae really have enough sockets for all this kit I'm installing here."

With a shock, Carol recognised the voice, although she hadn't heard it for so long. Wordlessly, she stepped over the protruding legs and moved over to the window. It was an old timber sash window, which she usually had to struggle with, even to raise it an inch. Today however, it fairly flew up, spraying flakes of old paint all over her blouse.

She brushed the paint from her and turned round. He was on his feet, watching her. He looked different somehow: he was always stocky, but now he looked a teeny bit overweight, although only by about half a stone, and his hairline was receding slightly, although only about half an inch, if that.

"Hello Jim. You're looking well."

"So are you Carol – you're looking great."

"SJM Business Solutions – I didn't know you were employed by them."

"I'm not."

"You're not? But that's the company we hired to put in the system …"

"Aye, but SJM Business Solutions *is* me, or strictly speaking me and Siobhan."

Siobhan, his wife. Carol had spoken to her on the phone, when she was discussing the quotation. She'd never let on who she was.

"Nobody wanted to hire an old guy like me when I left Uni, so I thought, let's just go for it, become self-employed. Anyway, I'd enough of working for a boss when I was a butcher."

"That's great Jim, I'm pleased for you. Is everything working out all right?"

"Aye, slow but sure. Networking, that's the buzz word these days, and I don't mean the computer systems. The Enterprise Company keeps sending me on courses to meet and greet, which has been OK really, got a few customers out of it."

"And Siobhan – I take it she's the S in the title?"

"Aye, insisted on coming first, typical woman."

Carol wasn't sure if he had meant the double entendre, but she blushed at the memories his words conjured. He looked at her quizzically, and the penny dropped.

"Ach, you know what I meant to say!"

He grinned mischievously at her, and she managed to find the strength to grin back.

"I know. How is she keeping anyway, feeling all right?"

He looked surprised.

"So you've heard about our unexpected expectancy?"

"Yes, Sarah told me."

Although strictly speaking it was Kathleen. Sarah had brought her up to see her Auntie Annie and Uncle Alistair, on a day that Carol had happened to be visiting. Josie was away for the day: everybody knew she was at Barlinnie Prison, spending time with Michael, but it was an unacknowledged rule that these outings were never referred to. As far as Sarah was concerned, Michael had ceased to exist, and Josie colluded with this fiction. It was the only way the two women were able to survive, to get on with their lives, although Kathleen helped to dull their pain.

Carol had taken the tot to the toilet. She had been helping her to pull her tights up, and had playfully remarked to her that she had a wee fat tummy.

"Yes, I've got a fat tummy 'cos Grannie keeps

feeding me mince and tatties. Grandpa says I'm going to burst like a balloon."

"Does he now? Cheek o' him! Wash your hands now sweetheart."

"But do you know, Auntie Siobhan's got the fattest tummy ever! She's got a baby growing in her!"

And that's how she'd found out. What had annoyed her was that no one had told her, neither Josie, Annie nor Sarah, and that made her suspect that they all thought she would be upset by the news, which of course she wasn't.

"It would've been better to wait until we'd established the business, but there you go, some things you just cannae plan for."

"It'll work out for the best. It always does," she took a deep breath, which nearly became a sigh. "Anyway, did you meet the office junior?"

"Aye, I did that! I thought he was still away in the clink, but instead he's next door, asking me to set up a time sheet for him. Life's full of surprises, eh?"

"You can say that again."

"Life's full of …"

She hit him with a folder. Not *too* hard.

"Heh, I thought you were anti-violence!"

"I've changed my mind over the years."

"Really? I've gone the other way. In fact the last bit of aggro I was in was that time with Eddie in 'The Spuig'."

She watched him as he screwed his eyes up,

realising what else had happened that afternoon. It was his turn to blush.

"Carol …"

"So, I hear you live in the West End now! You've gone a bit soft, joined the wine bar brigade! No wonder you've got a quieter life, you've become a trendy west-endie!"

He looked relieved.

"And you're still a born again Gorbalite?"

"I don't see me ever leaving the place."

"Josie still likes living there an' all … she keeps me up to date with how you're getting on, you know."

"So you must have known I had my own firm."

"I did, and I knew you'd hired us for your IT system."

"You were the cheapest quote."

"Your contract's a loss leader. Hopefully you'll tell all your friends about us."

A loss leader. Just waiting for the real thing to come along.

He had his jacket on now. She realised she'd never seen him in a suit before, maybe that was what made him look a bit stouter. He reached under the desk and pulled out his holdall – the same old faithful that had followed him around when they were together. It was looking a lot shabbier than he was.

"I always used to wonder what you kept in that bag."

"I should really have one of those briefcase

thingies, but I've grown attached to this old thing."

He pulled out a sheaf of papers.

"Sign here and here. Any problems, our phone number's on the documents. One phone call and I'll be back out."

She could tell him she was a techno phobic, and have him running after her on a weekly basis. He might even be fed up with his pregnant wife and welcome some out of hours frenzied shagging, over and under the desks.

She signed the documents and held them out to him.

"I'm sure it won't be necessary, Jim. I'm a bit of a whizz-kid with IT, and Patsy's even better. In fact, if you come back you might be tempted to headhunt her."

"It's as well that I stay away then."

She watched him put the paperwork away in old faithful. He still had a nice bum.

"Yes. It is."

It took him a while to get out of the office, with Patsy giving him an update on her ever expanding family, twenty-two nieces and nephews at the last count, and John insisting on giving him a 'tribal' hug. His arms only just managed to get round Jim's chest.

She watched out her window as he puttered away in his old banger. No wonder he hid it round the back. So, he was gone. Again. She pressed the intercom button, three … four times before there was an answer.

"Hullo, who's that?"

"John? It's me of course. Where's Patsy?"

"Away for a pish. I'm covering reception."

"I see," she sighed, "John, come through here and show me how to turn on this computer, would you?"

* * *

Carol's dad was standing out on the stairs with Uncle Dan. They were waiting for the bells, so they could first foot their families. Her dad had a bottle of whisky with him, in case Dan fancied a wee half, but he himself wasn't drinking, he'd promised his family and it was his New Year resolution.

"Aw mum!" *protested Robert.* "I want to wait with my dad. How can I no' go on the stairs?"

"You've got fair hair."

The look on Auntie Sarah's face said that this was the most obvious answer in the world.

Carol's mum was just finishing making up the tinned ham and tomato pieces, having put a few without tomatoes on a separate plate for Carol.

"Do you know Carol, see when I was a wee girl during the rationing, nobody had allergies. Why was that, I wonder?"

Carol rolled her eyes.

"Cos you were grateful for what you could get."

Robert was looking perplexed. "Fair hair? So what?"

"Right, cheeky madam, have you put those glasses out onto the sideboard?"

"Yes. And I've put out the crisps. And the nuts. Can I get something to drink?"

Robert wasn't giving up.

"Fair hair?"

Annie looked at Carol, and nodded over at her nephew, a smile spreading over her face.

"No' until your daddy arrives. Then you can get a wee Advocat and lemonade."

"I'd rather have a dry martini."

"We'll see."

Robert tried a different approach "I'll put my anorak on."

Carol looked at Annie and Sarah and then at Robert.

"You cannae go out, blondie, in case you're the first back in. You might be a Viking."

Robert looked at them.

"You two are taking the Mick."

"What an expression," answered Annie. "Anyway Robert, put the telly on, so we know when the New Year comes. Carol, go and bring Mrs Quinn through. She'll be sitting herself."

Carol went across the landing to her neighbour's flat. Mrs Quinn was sitting with her jacket on and a wee parcel of food and drink ready. She liked the old lady, so she played along with her when she looked surprised to be invited, and she even managed, with a straight face, to plead with Mrs Quinn not to see in the New Year in her bed.

They met her dad and Uncle Dan on the stairs when they were going back through.

"Hello, pet. Is that you gonnae join us, Mary? We'll need to plank the sherry!"

"Ah now, Archie, a wee glass'll do me!"

"That's no' whit I heard Mary! I heard you go to mass every day to tan that communion wine."

Archie actually meant no harm in saying this, but the old lady looked hurt. He looked sheepishly at Uncle Dan, who never spoke much. He looked straight back at Archie, expressionless.

"Ach, I'm only kiddin' hen. Away in oot the cauld and get a plate of Annie's soup."

They went back into Carol's home. It was nearly midnight. There was a lot of highland dancers on the television, and a man in a kilt singing "Donald, Where's Your Troosers" She'd never been up to the Highlands, but she was sure it was nothing like the telly made it out to be.

Midnight. The five of them counted down with the clangs of the bells on the telly. Twelve o'clock. They wished each other Happy New Year, Robert wiping his face after Mrs Quinn kissed him. Out of devilment, Carol made sure she gave Robert a great big kiss on the cheek, the kind with sound effects.

There was a knock at the door; it was her dad and Uncle Dan. More kissing and cuddling.

Drinks were poured, (a pint of coke for her dad). They tucked into the food and praised her mother's soup.

"What d'you make it with Annie?" asked Mrs Quinn, on her third bowl.

"A ham hough. They stock cubes are rubbish."

"That's very true Annie. It's a sin, right enough. Everything's out of packets these days. Do you know what Martin brought me the other day? A Pot Noodle!

Never heard of the likes."

"I had one in ma pals," Robert chimed in. "They're great!"

Auntie Sarah went out of the room and came back in holding Robert's accordion.

"Look what I found in the hall press," she grinned.

Archie looked at Robert. "The wee man's brought his accordion. Good on you!"

Robert looked embarrassed by all the attention. Carol knew his parents had made him bring the accordion.

"Give us Flower of Scotland!"

"Anarchy in the UK!"

"The Sash!" this last one was from Archie. It was met with a "wheesht" from his wife and a glance at Mrs Quinn.

Robert played Flower of Scotland, and then other tunes that he said were reels and jigs. Everyone danced up and down the living room, linking arms with each other. Nobody knew any real Highland dances, but they had lots of energy.

After twenty minutes of this, they all collapsed onto chairs exhausted. Mrs Quinn was still on her feet.

"When I was a wee lass in Donegal, I could jig through 'til dawn."

"Give us a song, Mary."

"Ah no, me singing voice is long gone."

"That's no' true. I hear you singin' in the bath!"

"Archie, you're a terror! Right, I'll give you a wee tune that I used to sing to me man. As you know, Mr Lawrence, he was named the same as yourself."

Mrs Quinn began to sing. She was a wee tiny lady,

and sang like a bird, she could hold a tune.

> *'Oh Danny boy, the pipes, the pipes are calling,*
> *From glen to glen and down the mountainside.*
> *The summer's gone, and all the roses falling,*
> *It's you, it's you must go, and I must bide.'*

Robert picked up the tune and played the accordion softly in the background. Everyone was completely still, listening to the song.

> *'But you come back when summer's in the meadow,*
> *Or when the valley's hushed and white with snow,*
> *It's I'll be here in sunshine or in shadow,*
> *Oh Danny boy, Oh Danny boy, I love you so.'*

Auntie Sarah grasped her husband's hand, a dreamy look on her face. He sat up straight and looked a bit embarrassed, but he didn't let go. Mrs Quinn sniffed and wiped her eye, laughing and crying. Her husband Daniel had died during the summer. They'd been married for fifty years and had been in the papers with all their children, grandchildren and great grandchildren.

"That was lovely Mrs Quinn," said Auntie Sarah, "you must miss your man terrible."

"Ah now Sarah dear! When you've a man, you've a master, and I'm quite glad to be rid of him."

Robert and Carol exploded with embarrassed mirth. Annie tutted at them, and aimed a skite at the top of Robert's head, as he was closest. He ducked and she missed, although she wasn't really trying very hard.

Auntie Sarah looked alarmed. Nobody ever hit her boy, not even a kid-on slap. To change the subject, Auntie Sarah turned to Carol.

"How do you like the big school now pet?"

"Yes, it's good. I don't like Physics but."

Annie jumped in. "She gets A's all the time. She's going to be a lawyer, you know."

Uncle Dan looked at her. He hadn't said much since he arrived, although he'd been up dancing with everyone else.

"You're a hard working lassie, Carol. We're all proud of you."

Carol was touched and amazed by this unexpected compliment. She blushed and smiled back to him.

"Right weans – aye, you're no' sixteen yet Carol - bedtime. The adults'll stay up a bit longer. Robert, I've made up the zed bed for you in Carol's room."

After some protests, they made for bed. Robert put his jammies on in the bathroom, and only came into the room when Carol was tucked up in bed. He fell asleep right away, snoring softly. There was something up with his nose and he couldn't breathe through it at night. The doctor said he was to get a wee operation but Auntie Sarah was too scared to let him.

The Martini, food and dancing had made Carol tired as well. As she felt herself drifting into sleep, she was happy. Her dad didn't drink and her mum didn't cry any more. Everything was going to be all right now. All her troubles were over.

Glossary

B

Ben Inside (a room)

Birl Twirl around (in a dance)

Brammed up Dressed up

Breenged Jumped

Bubbly-jocks Turkeys

Burd Woman, girlfriend

C

Close Passageway between tenement buildings which allowed access to the flats

Coorying To cuddle in

Coupon Face; expression

Cludgie Toilet; generally an outside toilet

D

Diddy Breast

Dobber A person of limited intellect (slang word for a penis)

Douts Cigarette ends

Dreepied Climbed down from

Dreich Wet and rainy

Drookit Drenched, soaked by rain or liquid

F

Fankle	Mix up
Flittin'	Moving house
Foosty	Stale, mouldy
Forbye	Besides
Fu'	Inebriated, as in 'full of drink'

G

Galloots	Idiots
Girnin'	Complaining, moaning, crying
Gret	Cried
Guddle	Mess, confusion

H

Hard ticket	Hard-faced woman
Hoaching	Heaving, busy (with people)
Hoor	Whore

J

Jaikey	A tramp, frequently drunk
Juke	Nip in or just go quickly
Jiggered	Done In. Exhausted

M

Mawkit	Filthy

N

Navvy	An Irish building worker

P

Pape	A catholic
Pelters	Extreme teasing, (a lot of)
Polis	Police
Puggled	Exhausted, done for or sometimes used as an expression for really drunk or drugged
Purvey	The tea or meal held after a funeral

R

Rammy	Fight

S

Sanferryan (to me)	It is of little consequence to me (a corruption of a French phrase)
Shebeen	An unlicensed drinking house
Sherricking	To be lambasted, severe telling off
Shoogle	Shake
Shugh	The space between the buttocks
Sined	A quick throwing of water on ones face
Skite	Swipe, skelp
Slunged	Another word for a quick throwing of water on ones face
Smout	Small person
Stookie	Plaster cast usually associated with broken limbs

Stotting	Bouncing
Stramash	Fight, fuss and bother
Swither	Debate one way or another
T	
Teenie	Very small
Thole	Put up with, endure
Thrawn	Stubborn
Tobered	To tober someone is to tame them, to make them behave appropriately
Trauchled	Troubled
Trogs	A group of youths, who have extremist views, can be violent and psychotic. The word derives from the word troglodyte which describes a cave-dweller or cave-man
Tumbling your wilkies	To tumble your body over like a ball
W	
Weans	Children
Wummen	Women